Penguin Books
Smart-Aleck Kill

One of the great writers of detective fiction, Raymond Chandler was born in Chicago in 1888. When he was twelve his family emigrated to England, where he was educated at Dulwich College. After studying in France and Germany he returned to London in 1907, where he reluctantly joined the Civil Service. He left to take up writing and worked for a number of newspapers as a reporter, essayist, book-reviewer and writer of verse. In 1912 he sailed to America and eventually settled in California. After the First World War, during which he served in the Canadian Army, he went into business and became a top executive for an oil company. In 1924 he married Cissy Pascal. With the onset of the Depression in the early thirties he returned to writing, producing stories for pulp magazines such as *Black Mask*. By 1938 he had published sixteen stories and was working on his first novel. *The Big Sleep*, which was published in 1939. An instant success, it introduced, in the words of one critic, 'a new type of crime novel in which ingenuity of plot and detection combine with a distinctive and distinguished literary style'. The success of his first book was matched by *Farewell, My Lovely* (1940), *The High Window* (1942), *The Lady in the Lake* (1943), *The Little Sister* (1949) and *The Long Good-Bye* (1954), all of which feature his famous private detective, Philip Marlowe. Many of his books have been made into highly successful feature films and he wrote screenplays for a number of films, including *Double Indemnity* and *The Blue Dahlia*, both of which were nominated for an Oscar. He was elected President of the Mystery Writers of America. During his later years he suffered increasingly from depression and general ill health and he died in 1959 in California. Dilys Powell called his writing a 'peculiar mixture of harshness, sensuality, high polish and backstreet poetry' and Elizabeth Bowen described him as 'a craftsman so brilliant, he had an imagination so wholly original, that no consideration of modern American literature ought . . . to exclude him'.

Raymond Chandler

Smart-Aleck Kill

Penguin Books
in association with Hamish Hamilton

PENGUIN BOOKS

Published by the Penguin Group
27 Wrights Lane, London w8 5tz, England
Viking Penguin Inc., 40 West 23rd Street, New York, New York 10010, USA
Penguin Books Australia Ltd, Ringwood, Victoria, Australia
Penguin Books Canada Ltd, 2801 John Street, Markham, Ontario, Canada l3r 1b4
Penguin Books (NZ) Ltd, 182–190 Wairau Road, Auckland 10, New Zealand

Penguin Books Ltd, Registered Offices: Harmondsworth, Middlesex, England

First published by Hamish Hamilton 1958
Published in Penguin Books 1964
10 9 8 7 6

The stories in this book are
taken from *The Simple Art of Murder*

Made and printed in Great Britain by
Richard Clay Ltd, Bungay, Suffolk
Set in Monotype Bembo

Contents

Smart-Aleck Kill

I

The doorman of the Kilmarnock was six foot two. He wore a pale blue uniform, and white gloves made his hands look enormous. He opened the door of the Yellow taxi as gently as an old maid stroking a cat.

Johnny Dalmas got out and turned to the red-haired driver. He said: 'Better wait for me around the corner, Joey.'

The driver nodded, tucked a toothpick a little farther back in the corner of his mouth, and swung his cab expertly away from the white-marked loading zone. Dalmas crossed the sunny sidewalk and went into the enormous cool lobby of the Kilmarnock. The carpets were thick, soundless. Bellboys stood with folded arms and the two clerks behind the marble desk looked austere.

Dalmas went across to the elevator lobby. He got into a panelled car and said: 'End of the line, please.'

The penthouse floor had a small quiet lobby with three doors opening off it, one to each wall. Dalmas crossed to one of them and rang the bell.

Derek Walden opened the door. He was about forty-five, possibly a little more, and had a lot of powdery grey hair and a handsome, dissipated face that was beginning to go pouchy. He had on a monogrammed lounging robe, and a glass full of whisky in his hand. He was a little drunk.

He said thickly, morosely: 'Oh, it's you. C'mon in, Dalmas.'

He went back into the apartment, leaving the door open.

Dalmas shut it and followed him into a long, high-ceilinged room with a balcony at one end and a line of french windows along the left side. There was a terrace outside.

Derek Walden sat down in a brown and gold chair against the wall and stretched his legs across a footstool. He swirled the whisky around in his glass, looking down at it.

'What's on your mind?' he asked.

Dalmas stared at him a little grimly. After a moment he said: 'I dropped in to tell you I'm giving you back your job.'

Walden drank the whisky out of his glass and put it down on the corner of a table. He fumbled around for a cigarette, stuck it in his mouth and forgot to light it.

'That so?' His voice was blurred but indifferent.

Dalmas turned away from him and walked over to one of the windows. It was open and an awning flapped outside. The traffic noise from the boulevard was faint.

He spoke over his shoulder:

'The investigation isn't getting anywhere – because you don't want it to get anywhere. *You* know why you're being blackmailed. *I* don't. Eclipse Films is interested because they have a lot of sugar tied up in films you have made.'

'To hell with Eclipse Films,' Walden said, almost quietly.

Dalmas shook his head and turned around. 'Not from my angle. They stand to lose if you get in a jam the publicity hounds can't handle. You took me on because you were asked to. It was a waste of time. You haven't co-operated worth a cent.'

Walden said in an unpleasant tone: 'I'm handling this my own way and I'm not gettin' into any jam. I'll make my own deal – when I can buy something that'll stay bought. . . . And all you have to do is make the Eclipse people think the situation's bein' taken care of. That clear?'

Dalmas came part-way back across the room. He stood with one hand on top of a table, beside an ashtray littered with cigarette stubs that had very dark lip rouge on them. He looked down at these absently.

'That wasn't explained to me, Walden,' he said coldly.

'I thought you were smart enough to figure it out,' Walden sneered. He leaned sidewise and slopped some more whisky into his glass. 'Have a drink?'

Dalmas said: 'No, thanks.'

Walden found the cigarette in his mouth and threw it on the floor. He drank. 'What the hell!' he snorted. 'You're a private detective and you're being paid to make a few motions that don't mean anything. It's a clean job – as your racket goes.'

Dalmas said: 'That's another crack I could do without hearing.'

Walden made an abrupt, angry motion. His eyes glittered. The corners of his mouth drew down and his face got sulky. He avoided Dalmas' stare.

Dalmas said: 'I'm not against you, but I never was for you. You're not the kind of guy I could go for, ever. If you had played with me, I'd have done what I could. I still will – but not for your sake. I don't want your money – and you can pull your shadows off my tail any time you like.'

Walden put his feet on the floor. He laid his glass down very carefully on the table at his elbow. The whole expression of his face changed.

'Shadows? . . . I don't get you.' He swallowed. 'I'm not having you shadowed.'

Dalmas stared at him. After a moment he nodded. 'Okay, then. I'll backtrack on the next one and see if I can make him tell who he's working for . . . I'll find out.'

Walden said very quietly: 'I wouldn't do that, if I were you. You're – you're monkeying with people that might get nasty . . . I know what I'm talking about.'

'That's something I'm not going to let worry me,' Dalmas said evenly. 'If it's the people that want *your* money, they were nasty a long time ago.'

He held his hat out in front of him and looked at it. Walden's face glistened with sweat. His eyes looked sick. He opened his mouth to say something.

The door buzzer sounded.

Walden scowled quickly, swore. He stared down the room but did not move.

'Too damn many people come here without bein' announced,' he growled. 'My Jap boy is off for the day.'

The buzzer sounded again, and Walden started to get up. Dalmas said: 'I'll see what it is. I'm on my way anyhow.'

He nodded to Walden, went down the room, and opened the door.

Two men came in with guns in their hands. One of the guns dug sharply into Dalmas' ribs, and the man who was holding it said urgently: 'Back up, and make it snappy. This is one of those stick-ups you read about.'

He was dark and good-looking and cheerful. His face was as clear as a cameo, almost without hardness. He smiled.

The one behind him was short and sandy-haired. He scowled. The dark one said: 'This is Walden's dick, Noddy. Take him over and go through him for a gun.'

The sandy-haired man, Noddy, put a short-barrelled revolver against Dalmas' stomach and his partner kicked the door shut, then strolled carelessly down the room towards Walden.

Noddy took a .38 Colt from under Dalmas' arm, walked around him and tapped his pockets. He put his own gun away and transferred Dalmas' Colt to his business hand.

'Okay, Ricchio. This one's clean,' he said in a grumbling voice. Dalmas let his arms fall, turned, and went back into the room. He looked thoughtfully at Walden. Walden was leaning forward with his mouth open and an expression of intense concentration on his face. Dalmas looked at the dark stick-up and said softly: 'Ricchio?'

The dark boy glanced at him. 'Over there by the table, sweetheart. I'll do all the talkin'.'

Walden made a hoarse sound in his throat. Ricchio stood in front of him, looking down at him pleasantly, his gun dangling from one finger by the trigger guard.

'You're too slow on the pay-off, Walden. Too damn slow!

So we came to tell you about it. Tailed your dick here too. Wasn't that cute?'

Dalmas said gravely, quietly: 'This punk used to be your bodyguard, Walden – if his name is Ricchio.'

Walden nodded silently and licked his lips. Ricchio snarled at Dalmas: 'Don't crack wise, dick. I'm tellin' you again.' He stared with hot eyes, then looked back at Walden, looked at a watch on his wrist.

'It's eight minutes past three, Walden. I figure a guy with your drag can still get dough out of the bank. We're giving you an hour to raise ten grand. Just an hour. And we're takin' your shamus along to arrange about delivery.'

Walden nodded again, still silent. He put his hands down on his knees and clutched them until his knuckles whitened.

Ricchio went on: 'We'll play clean. Our racket wouldn't be worth a squashed bug if we didn't. You'll play clean too. If you don't your shamus will wake up on a pile of dirt. Only he won't wake up. Get it?'

Dalmas said contemptuously: 'And if he pays up – I suppose you turn me loose to put the finger on you.'

Smoothly, without looking at him, Ricchio said: 'There's an answer to that one, too. . . . Ten grand to-day, Walden. The other ten grand the first of the week. Unless we have trouble, . . . If we do, we'll get paid for our trouble.'

Walden made an aimless, defeated gesture with both hands outspread. 'I guess I can arrange it,' he said hurriedly.

'Swell. We'll be on our way then.'

Ricchio nodded shortly and put his gun away. He took a brown kid glove out of his pocket, put it on his right hand, moved across, then took Dalmas' Colt away from the sandy-haired man. He looked it over, slipped it into his side pocket and held it there with the gloved hand.

'Let's drift,' he said with a jerk of his head.

They went out. Derek Walden stared after them bleakly.

The elevator car was empty except for the operator. They got off at the mezzanine and went across a silent writing room past a stained-glass window with lights behind it to give the effect of sunshine. Ricchio walked half a step behind on Dalmas' left. The sandy-haired man was on his right, crowding him.

They went down carpeted steps to an arcade of luxury shops, along that, out of the hotel through the side entrance. A small brown sedan was parked across the street. The sandy-haired man slid behind the wheel, stuck his gun under his leg and stepped on the starter. Ricchio and Dalmas got in the back. Ricchio drawled: 'East on the boulevard, Noddy. I've got to figure.'

Noddy grunted. 'That's a kick,' he growled over his shoulder. 'Ridin' a guy down Wilshire in daylight.'

'Drive the heap, bozo.'

The sandy-haired man grunted again and drove the small sedan away from the kerb, slowed a moment later for the boulevard stop. An empty Yellow pulled away from the west kerb, swung around in the middle of the block and fell in behind. Noddy made his stop, turned right and went on. The taxi did the same. Ricchio glanced back at it without interest. There was a lot of traffic on Wilshire.

Dalmas leaned back against the upholstery and said thoughtfully: 'Why wouldn't Walden use his telephone while we were coming down?'

Ricchio smiled at him. He took his hat off and dropped it in his lap, then took his right hand out of his pocket and held it under the hat with the gun in it.

'He wouldn't want us to get mad at him, dick.'

'So he lets a couple of punks take me for the ride.'

Ricchio said coldly: 'It's not that kind of a ride. We need you in our business. . . . And we ain't punks, see?'

Dalmas rubbed his jaw with a couple of fingers. He smiled slightly, said nothing. The sandy-haired man turned his head quickly and snapped: 'Straight ahead at Robertson?'

'Yeah. I'm still figuring,' Ricchio said.

'What a brain!' the sandy-haired man sneered.

Ricchio grinned tightly and showed even white teeth. The light changed to red half a block ahead. Noddy slid the sedan forward and was first in the line at the intersection. The empty Yellow drifted up on his left. Not quite level. The driver of it had red hair. His cap was balanced on one side of his head and he whistled cheerfully past a toothpick.

Dalmas drew his feet back against the seat and put his weight on them. He pressed his back hard against the upholstery. The tall traffic light went green and the sedan started forward, then hung a moment for a car that crowded into a fast left turn. The Yellow slipped forward on the left and the red-haired driver leaned over his wheel, yanked it suddenly to the right. There was a grinding, tearing noise. The riveted fender of the taxi ploughed over the low-swung fender of the brown sedan, locked over its left front wheel. The two cars jolted to a stop.

Horn blasts behind the two cars sounded angrily, impatiently.

Dalmas' right fist crashed against Ricchio's jaw. His left hand closed over the gun in Ricchio's lap. He jerked it loose as Ricchio sagged in the corner. Ricchio's head wobbled. His eyes opened and shut flickeringly. Dalmas slid away from him along the seat and slipped the Colt under his arm.

Noddy was sitting quite still in the front seat. His right hand moved slowly towards the gun under his thigh. Dalmas opened the door of the sedan and got out, shut the door, took two steps and opened the door of the taxi. He stood beside the taxi and watched the sandy-haired man.

Horns of the stalled cars blared furiously. The driver of the Yellow was out in front tugging at the two cars with a great show of energy and with no result at all. His toothpick waggled up and down in his mouth. A motor-cycle officer in amber glasses threaded the traffic, looked the situation over wearily, jerked his head at the driver.

'Get in and back up,' he advised. 'Argue it out somewhere else – we use this intersection.'

The driver grinned and scuttled around the front end of his

Yellow. He climbed into it, threw it in gear and worried it backwards with a lot of tooting and arm-waving. It came clear. The sandy-haired man peered woodenly from the sedan. Dalmas got into the taxi and pulled the door shut.

The motor-cycle officer drew a whistle out and blew two sharp blasts on it, spread his arms from east to west. The brown sedan went through the intersection like a cat chased by a police dog.

The Yellow went after it. Half a block on, Dalmas leaned forward and tapped on the glass.

'Let 'em go, Joey. You can't catch them and I don't want them. . . . That was a swell routine back there.'

The redhead leaned his chin towards the opening in the panel. 'Cinch, chief,' he said, grinning. 'Try me on a hard one some time.'

2

The telephone rang at twenty minutes to five. Dalmas was lying on his back on the bed. He was in his room at the Merrivale. He reached for the phone without looking at it, said: 'Hello.'

The girl's voice was pleasant and a little strained. 'This is Mianne Crayle. Remember?'

Dalmas took a cigarette from between his lips. 'Yes, Miss Crayle.'

'Listen. You must please go over and see Derek Walden. He's worried stiff about something and he's drinking himself blind. Something's got to be done.'

Dalmas stared past the phone at the ceiling. The hand holding his cigarette beat a tattoo on the side of the bed. He said slowly: 'He doesn't answer his phone, Miss Crayle. I've tried to call him a time or two.'

There was a short silence at the other end of the line. Then the voice said: 'I left my key under the door. You'd better just go on in.'

Dalmas' eyes narrowed. The fingers of his right hand became

still. He said slowly: 'I'll get over there right away, Miss Crayle. Where can I reach you?'

'I'm not sure.... At John Sutro's, perhaps. We were supposed to go there.'

Dalmas said: 'That's fine.' He waited for the click, then hung up and put the phone away on the night table. He sat up on the side of the bed and stared at a patch of sunlight on the wall for a minute or two. Then he shrugged, stood up. He finished a drink that stood beside the telephone, put on his hat, went down in the elevator and got into the second taxi in the line outside the hotel.

'Kilmarnock again, Joey. Step on it.'

It took fifteen minutes to get to the Kilmarnock.

The tea dance had let out and the streets around the big hotel were a mass of cars bucking their way out from the three entrances. Dalmas got out of the taxi half a block away and walked past groups of flushed débutantes and their escorts to the arcade entrance. He went in, walked up the stairs to the mezzanine, crossed the writing-room and got into an elevator full of people. They all got out before the penthouse floor.

Dalmas rang Walden's bell twice. Then he bent over and looked under the door. There was a fine thread of light broken by an obstruction. He looked back at the elevator indicators, then stooped and teased something out from under the door with the blade of a penknife. It was a flat key. He went in with it . . . stopped . . . stared. . . .

There was death in the big room. Dalmas went towards it slowly, walking softly, listening. There was a hard light in his grey eyes and the bone of his jaw made a sharp line that was pale against the tan of his cheek.

Derek Walden was slumped almost casually in the brown and gold chair. His mouth was slightly open. There was a blackened hole in his right temple, and a lacy pattern of blood spread down the side of his face and across the hollow of his neck as far as the soft collar of his shirt. His right hand trailed in the thick nap of the rug. The fingers held a small, black automatic.

The daylight was beginning to fade in the room. Dalmas stood perfectly still and stared at Derek Walden for a long time. There was no sound anywhere. The breeze had gone down and the awnings outside the french windows were still.

Dalmas took a pair of thin suède gloves from his left hip pocket and drew them on. He kneeled on the rug beside Walden and gently eased the gun from the clasp of his stiffening fingers. It was a .32, with a walnut grip, a black finish. He turned it over and looked at the stock. His mouth tightened. The number had been filed off and the patch of file marks glistened faintly against the dull black of the finish. He put the gun down on the rug and stood up, walked slowly towards the telephone that was on the end of a library table, beside a flat bowl of cut flowers.

He put his hand towards the phone but didn't touch it. He let the hand fall to his side. He stood there a moment, then turned and went quickly back and picked up the gun again. He slipped the magazine out and ejected the shell that was in the breech, picked that up, and pressed it into the magazine. He forked two fingers of his left hand over the barrel, held the cocking piece back, twisted the breech block, and broke the gun apart. He took the butt piece over to the window.

The number that was duplicated on the inside of the stock had not been filed off.

He reassembled the gun quickly, put the empty shell into the chamber, pushed the magazine home, cocked the gun and fitted it back into Derek Walden's dead hand. He pulled the suède gloves off his hands and wrote the number down in a small notebook.

He left the apartment, went down in the elevator, left the hotel. It was half past five and some of the cars on the boulevard had switched on their lights.

3

The blond man who opened the door at Sutro's did it very thoroughly. The door crashed back against the wall and the blond man sat down on the floor – still holding on to the knob. He said indignantly: 'Earthquake, by gad!'

Dalmas looked down at him without amusement.

'Is Miss Mianne Crayle here – or wouldn't you know?' he asked.

The blond man got off the floor and hurled the door away from him. It went shut with another crash. He said in a loud voice: 'Everybody's here but the Pope's tomcat – and he's expected.'

Dalmas nodded. 'You ought to have a swell party.'

He went past the blond man down the hall and turned under an arch into a big old-fashioned room with built-in china closets and a lot of shabby furniture. There were seven or eight people in the room and they were all flushed with liquor.

A girl in shorts and a green polo shirt was shooting craps on the floor with a man in dinner clothes. A fat man with pince-nez was talking sternly into a toy telephone. He was saying: 'Long Distance – Sioux City – and put some snap into it, sister!'

The radio blared 'Sweet Madness'.

Two couples were dancing around carelessly bumping into each other and the furniture. A man who looked like Al Smith was dancing all alone, with a drink in his hand and an absent expression on his face. A tall, white-faced blonde weaved towards Dalmas, slopping liquor out of her glass. She shrieked: 'Darling! Fancy meeting you here!'

Dalmas went around her, went towards a saffron-coloured woman who had just come into the room with a bottle of gin in each hand. She put the bottles on the piano and leaned against it, looking bored. Dalmas went up to her and asked for Miss Crayle.

The saffron-coloured woman reached a cigarette out of an open box on the piano. 'Outside – in the yard,' she said tonelessly.

Dalmas said: 'Thank you, Mrs Sutro.'

She stared at him blankly. He went under another arch, into

a darkened room with wicker furniture in it. A door led to a glassed-in porch and a door out of that led down steps to a path that wound off through dim trees. Dalmas followed the path to the edge of a bluff that looked out over the lighted part of Hollywood. There was a stone seat at the edge of the bluff. A girl sat on it with her back to the house. A cigarette tip glowed in the darkness. She turned her head slowly and stood up.

She was small and dark and delicately made. Her mouth showed dark with rouge, but there was not enough light to see her face clearly. Her eyes were shadowed.

Dalmas said: 'I have a cab outside, Miss Crayle. Or did you bring a car?'

'No car. Let's go. It's rotten here, and I don't drink gin.'

They went back along the path and passed around the side of the house. A trellis-topped gate let them out on the sidewalk, and they went along by the fence to where the taxi was waiting. The driver was leaning against it with one heel hooked on the edge of the running board. He opened the cab door. They got in.

Dalmas said: 'Stop at a drugstore for some butts, Joey.'

'Oke.'

Joey slid behind his wheel and started up. The cab went down a steep, winding hill. There was a little moisture on the surface of the asphalt pavement and the store fronts echoed back the swishing sound of the tyres.

After a while Dalmas said: 'What time did you leave Walden?'

The girl spoke without turning her head towards him. 'About three o'clock.'

'Put it a little later, Miss Crayle. He was alive at three o'clock – and there was somebody else with him.'

The girl made a small, miserable sound like a strangled sob. Then she said very softly: 'I know . . . he's dead.' She lifted her gloved hands and pressed them against her temples.

Dalmas said: 'Sure. Let's not get any more tricky than we have to. . . . Maybe we'll have to – enough.'

She said very slowly, in a low voice: 'I was there after he was dead.'

Dalmas nodded. He did not look at her. The cab went on and after a while it stopped in front of a corner drugstore. The driver turned in his seat and looked back. Dalmas stared at him, but spoke to the girl.

'You ought to have told me more over the phone. I might have got in a hell of a jam. I may be in a hell of a jam now.'

The girl swayed forward and started to fall. Dalmas put his arm out quickly and caught her, pushed her back against the cushions. Her head wobbled on her shoulders and her mouth was a dark gash in her stone-white face. Dalmas held her shoulder and felt her pulse with his free hand. He said sharply, grimly: 'Let's go on to Carli's, Joey. Never mind the butts. . . . This party has to have a drink – in a hurry.'

Joey slammed the cab in gear and stepped on the accelerator.

4

Carli's was a small club at the end of a passage between a sporting-goods store and a circulating library. There was a grilled door and a man behind it who had given up trying to look as if it mattered who came in.

Dalmas and the girl sat in a small booth with hard seats and looped-back green curtains. There were high partitions between the booths. There was a long bar down the other side of the room and a big juke box at the end of it. Now and then, when there wasn't enough noise, the bartender put a nickel in the juke box.

The waiter put two small glasses of brandy on the table and Mianne Crayle downed hers at a gulp. A little light came into her shadowed eyes. She peeled a black and white gauntlet off her right hand and sat playing with the empty fingers of it, staring down at the table. After a little while the waiter came back with a couple of brandy highballs.

When he had gone away again Mianne Crayle began to speak in a low, clear voice, without raising her head: 'I wasn't the first of his women by several dozen. I wouldn't have been the last – by that many more. But he had his decent side. And believe it or not he didn't pay my room rent.'

Dalmas nodded, didn't say anything. The girl went on without looking at him: 'He was a heel in a lot of ways. When he was sober he had the dark blue sulks. When he was lit up he was vile. When he was nicely edged he was a pretty good sort of guy besides being the best smut director in Hollywood. He could get more smooth sexy tripe past the Hays office than any other three men.'

Dalmas said without expression: 'He was on his way out. Smut is on its way out, and that was all he knew.'

The girl looked at him briefly, lowered her eyes again and drank a little of her highball. She took a tiny handkerchief out of the pocket of her sports jacket and patted her lips.

The people on the other side of the partition were making a great deal of noise.

Mianne Crayle said: 'We had lunch on the balcony. Derek was drunk and on the way to get drunker. He had something on his mind. Something that worried him a lot.'

Dalmas smiled faintly. 'Maybe it was the twenty grand somebody was trying to prise loose from him – or didn't you know about that?'

'It might have been that. Derek was a bit tight about money.'

'His liquor cost him a lot,' Dalmas said dryly. 'And that motor cruiser he liked to play about in – down below the border.'

The girl lifted her head with a quick jerk. There were sharp lights of pain in her dark eyes. She said very slowly: 'He bought all his liquor at Ensenada. Brought it in himself. He had to be careful – with the quantity he put away.'

Dalmas nodded. A cold smile played about the corners of his mouth. He finished his drink and put a cigarette in his mouth, felt in his pocket for a match. The holder on the table was empty.

'Finish your story, Miss Crayle,' he said.

'We went up to the apartment. He got two fresh bottles out and said he was going to get good and drunk.... Then we quarrelled ... I couldn't stand any more of it. I went away. When I got home I began to worry about him. I called up but he wouldn't answer the phone. I went back finally ... and let myself in with the key I had ... and he was dead in the chair.'

After a moment Dalmas said: 'Why didn't you tell me some of that over the phone?'

She pressed the heels of her hands together, said very softly: 'I was terribly afraid.... And there was something ... wrong.'

Dalmas put his head back against the partition, stared at her with his eyes half closed.

'It's an old gag,' she said. 'I'm almost ashamed to spring it. But Derek Walden was left-handed ... I'd know about that, wouldn't I?'

Dalmas said very softly: 'A lot of people must have known that – but one of them might have got careless.'

Dalmas stared at Mianne Crayle's empty glove. She was twisting it between her fingers.

'Walden was left-handed,' he said slowly. 'That means he didn't suicide. The gun was in his other hand. There was no sign of a struggle and the hole in his temple was powder-burned, looked as if the shot came from about the right angle. That means whoever shot him was someone who could get in there and get close to him. Or else he was paralysed drunk, and in that case whoever did it had to have a key.'

Mianne Crayle pushed the glove away from her. She clenched her hands. 'Don't make it any plainer,' she said sharply. 'I know the police will think I did it. Well – I didn't. I loved the poor damn fool. What do you think of that?'

Dalmas said without emotion: 'You *could* have done it, Miss Crayle. They'll think of that, won't they? And you might be smart enough to act the way you have afterwards. They'll think of that, too.'

'That wouldn't be smart,' she said bitterly. 'Just smart-aleck.'

'Smart-aleck kill!' Dalmas laughed grimly. 'Not bad.' He ran his fingers through his crisp hair. 'No, I don't think we can pin it on you – and maybe the cops won't know he was left-handed ... until somebody else gets a chance to find things out.'

He leaned over the table a little, put his hands on the edge as if to get up. His eyes narrowed thoughtfully on her face.

'There's one man downtown that might give me a break. He's all cop, but he's an old guy and don't give a damn about his publicity. Maybe if you went down with me, let him size you up and hear the story, he'd stall the case a few hours and hold out on the papers.'

He looked at her questioningly. She drew her glove on and said quietly: 'Let's go.'

5

When the elevator doors at the Merrivale closed, the big man put his newspaper down from in front of his face and yawned. He got up slowly from the settee in the corner and loafed across the small but sedate lobby. He squeezed himself into a booth at the end of a row of house phones. He dropped a coin in the slot and dialled with a thick forefinger, forming the number with his lips.

After a pause he leaned close to the mouthpiece and said: 'This is Denny. I'm at the Merrivale. Our man just came in. I lost him outside and came here to wait for him to get back.'

He had a heavy voice with a burr in it. He listened to the voice at the other end, nodded and hung up without saying anything more. He went out of the booth, crossed to the elevators. On the way he dropped a cigar butt into a glazed jar full of white sand.

In the elevator he said: 'Ten,' and took his hat off. He had straight black hair that was damp with perspiration, a wide, flat face and small eyes. His clothes were unpressed, but not shabby. He was a studio dick and he worked for Eclipse Films.

He got out at the tenth floor and went along a dim corridor, turned a corner and knocked at a door. There was a sound of steps inside. The door opened. Dalmas opened it.

The big man went in, dropped his hat casually on the bed, sat down in an easy chair by the window without being asked.

He said: 'Hi, boy. I hear you need some help.'

Dalmas looked at him for a moment, without answering. Then he said slowly, frowningly: 'Maybe – for a tail. I asked for Collins. I thought you'd be too easy to spot.'

He turned away and went into the bathroom, came out with two glasses. He mixed the drinks on the bureau, handed one. The big man drank, smacked his lips and put his glass down on the sill of the open window. He took a short, chubby cigar out of his vest pocket.

'Collins wasn't around,' he said. 'And I was just countin' my thumbs. So the big cheese give me the job. Is it footwork?'

'I don't know. Probably not,' Dalmas said indifferently.

'If it's a tail in a car, I'm okay. I brought my little coupé.'

Dalmas took his glass and sat down on the side of the bed. He stared at the big man with a faint smile. The big man bit the end off his cigar and spat it out. Then he bent over and picked up the piece, looked at it, tossed it out of the window.

'It's a swell night. A bit warm for so late in the year,' he said.

Dalmas said slowly: 'How well do you know Derek Walden, Denny?'

Denny looked out of the window. There was a sort of haze in the sky and the reflection of a red neon sign behind a nearby building looked like a fire.

He said: 'I don't what you call know him. I've seen him around. I know he's one of the big money guys on the lot.'

'Then you won't fall over if I tell you he's dead,' Dalmas said evenly.

Denny turned around slowly. The cigar, still unlighted, moved up and down in his wide mouth. He looked mildly interested.

Dalmas went on: 'It's a funny one. A blackmail gang has

been working on him, Denny. Looks like it got his goat. He's dead – with a hole in his head and a gun in his hand. It happened this afternoon.'

Denny opened his small eyes a little wider. Dalmas sipped his drink and rested the glass on his thigh.

'His girl friend found him. She had a key to the apartment in the Kilmarnock. The Jap boy was away and that's all the help he kept. The gal didn't tell anyone. She beat it and called me up. I went over . . . I didn't tell anybody either.'

The big man said very slowly: 'For Pete's sake! The cops'll stick it into you and break it off, brother. You can't get away with that stuff.'

Dalmas stared at him, then turned his head away and stared at a picture on the wall. He said coldly: 'I'm doing it – and you're helping me. We've got a job, and a damn powerful organization behind us. There's a lot of sugar at stake.'

'How do you figure?' Denny asked grimly. He didn't look pleased.

'The girl friend doesn't think Walden suicided, Denny. I don't either, and I've got a sort of lead. But it has to be worked fast, because it's as good a lead for the law as us. I didn't expect to be able to check it right away, but I got a break.'

Denny said: 'Uh-huh. Don't make it too clever. I'm a slow thinker.'

He struck a match and lit his cigar. His hand shook just a little.

Dalmas said: 'It's not clever. It's kind of dumb. The gun that killed Walden is a filed gun. But I broke it and the inside number wasn't filed. And Headquarters has the number, in the special permits.'

'And you just went in and asked for it and they gave it to you,' Denny said grimly. 'And when they pick Walden up and trace the gun themselves, they'll just think it was swell of you to beat them to it.' He made a harsh noise in his throat.

Dalmas said: 'Take it easy, boy. The guy that did the checking rates. I don't have to worry about that.'

'Like hell you don't! And what would a guy like Walden be doin' with a filed gun? That's a felony rap.'

Dalmas finished his drink and carried his empty glass over to the bureau. He held the whisky bottle out. Denny shook his head. He looked very disgusted.

'If he had the gun, he might not have known about that, Denny. And it could be that it wasn't his gun at all. If it was a killer's gun, then the killer was an amateur. A professional wouldn't have that kind of artillery.'

The big man said slowly: 'Okay, what you get on the rod?'

Dalmas sat down on the bed again. He dug a package of cigarettes out of his pocket, lit one, and leaned forward to toss the match through the open window. He said: 'The permit was issued about a year ago to a newshawk on the *Press-Chronicle*, name of Dart Burwand. This Burwand was bumped off last April on the ramp of the Arcade Depot. He was all set to leave town, but he didn't make it. They never cracked the case, but the hunch is that this Burwand was tied to some racket – like the Lingle killing in Chi – and that he tried to shake one of the big boys. The big boy backfired on the idea. Exit Burwand.'

The big man was breathing deeply. He had let his cigar go out. Dalmas watched him gravely while he talked.

'I got that from Westfalls, on the *Press-Chronicle*,' Dalmas said. 'He's a friend of mine. There's more of it. This gun was given back to Burwand's wife – probably. She still lives here – out on North Kenmore. She might tell me what she did with the gun … and she might be tied to some racket herself, Denny. In that case she wouldn't tell me, but after I talk to her she might make some contacts we ought to know about. Get the idea?'

Denny struck another match and held it on the end of his cigar. His voice said thickly: 'What do I do – tail the broad after you put the idea to her, about the gun?'

'Right.'

The big man stood up, pretended to yawn. 'Can do,' he

grunted. 'But why all the hush-hush about Walden? Why not let the cops work it out? We're just goin' to get ourselves a lot of bad marks at Headquarters.'

Dalmas said slowly: 'It's got to be risked. We don't know what the blackmail crowd had on Walden, and the studio stands to lose too much money if it comes out in the investigation and gets a front-page spread all over the country.'

Denny said: 'You talk like Walden was spelled Valentino. Hell, the guy's only a director. All they got to do is take his name off a couple of unreleased pictures.'

'They figure different,' Dalmas said. 'But maybe that's because they haven't talked to you.'

Denny said roughly: 'Okay. But me, I'd let the girl friend take the damn rap! All the law ever wants is a fall guy.'

He went around the bed to get his hat, crammed it on his head.

'Swell,' he said sourly. 'We gotta find out all about it before the cops even know Walden is dead.' He gestured with one hand and laughed mirthlessly. 'Like they do in the movies.'

Dalmas put the whisky bottle away in the bureau drawer and put his hat on. He opened the door and stood aside for Denny to go out. He switched off the lights.

It was ten minutes to nine.

6

The tall blonde looked at Dalmas out of greenish eyes with very small pupils. He went in past her quickly, without seeming to move quickly. He pushed the door shut with his elbow.

He said: 'I'm a dick – private – Mrs Burwand. Trying to dig up a little dope you might know about.'

The blonde said: 'The name is Dalton, Helen Dalton. Forget the Burwand stuff.'

Dalmas smiled and said: 'I'm sorry. I should have known.'

The blonde shrugged her shoulders and drifted away from the door. She sat down on the edge of a chair that had a cigarette burn on the arm. The room was a furnished-apartment living-room with a lot of department-store bric-à-brac spread around. Two floor lamps burned. There were flounced pillows on the floor, a French doll sprawled against the base of one lamp, and a row of gaudy novels went across the mantel above the gas fire.

Dalmas said politely, swinging his hat: 'It's about a gun Dart Burwand used to own. It's showed up on a case I'm working on. I'm trying to trace it – from the time you had it.'

Helen Dalton scratched the upper part of her arm. She had half-inch-long fingernails. She said curtly: 'I don't have an idea what you're talking about.'

Dalmas stared at her and leaned against the wall. His voice got on edge.

'Maybe you remember that you used to be married to Dart Burwand and that he got bumped off last April. . . . Or is that too far back?'

The blonde bit one of her knuckles and said: 'Smart guy, huh?'

'Not unless I have to be. But don't fall asleep from that last shot in the arm.'

Helen Dalton sat up very straight, suddenly. All the vagueness went out of her expression. She spoke between tight lips.

'What's the howl about the gun?'

'It killed a guy, that's all,' Dalmas said carelessly.

She stared at him. After a moment she said: 'I was broke. I hocked it. I never got it out. I had a husband that made sixty bucks a week but didn't spend any of it on me. I never had a dime.'

Dalmas nodded. 'Remember the pawnshop where you left it?' he asked. 'Or maybe you still have the ticket.'

'No. It was on Main. The street's lined with them. And I don't have the ticket.'

Dalmas said: 'I was afraid of that.'

He walked slowly across the room, looked at the titles of some of the books on the mantel. He went on and stood in front of a small folding desk. There was a photo in a silver frame on the desk. Dalmas stared at it for some time. He turned slowly.

'It's too bad about the gun, Helen. A pretty important name was rubbed out with it this afternoon. The number was filed off the outside. If you hocked it, I'd figure some hood bought it from the hock-shop guy, except that a hood wouldn't file a gun that way. He'd know there was another number inside. So it wasn't a hood – and the man it was found with wouldn't be likely to get a gun in a hock shop.'

The blonde stood up slowly. Red spots burned in her cheeks. Her arms were rigid at her sides and her breath whispered. She said slowly, strainedly: 'You can't maul me around, dick. I don't want any part of any police business – and I've got some good friends to take care of me. Better scram.'

Dalmas looked back towards the frame on the desk. He said: 'Johnny Sutro oughtn't to leave his mug around in a broad's apartment that way. Somebody might think he was cheating.'

The blonde walked stiff-legged across the room and slammed the photo into the drawer of the desk. She slammed the drawer shut, and leaned her hips against the desk.

'You're all wet, shamus. That's not anybody called Sutro. Get on out, will you, for gawd's sake?'

Dalmas laughed unpleasantly. 'I saw you at Sutro's house this afternoon. You were so drunk you don't remember.'

The blonde made a movement as though she were going to the door. It opened and a man came in. He stood just inside the door and pushed it shut very slowly. His right hand was in the pocket of a light tweed overcoat. He was dark-skinned, high-shouldered, angular, with a sharp nose and chin.

Dalmas looked at him quietly and said: 'Good evening. Councilman Sutro.'

The man looked past Dalmas at the girl. He took no notice of Dalmas. The girl said shakily: 'This guy says he's a dick. He's giving me a third about some gun he says I had. Throw him out, will you?'

Sutro said: 'A dick, eh?'

He walked past Dalmas without looking at him. The blonde

backed away from him and fell into a chair. Her face got a pasty look and her eyes were scared. Sutro looked down at her for a moment, then turned around and took a small automatic out of his pocket. He held it loosely, pointed down at the floor.

He said: 'I haven't a lot of time.'

Dalmas said: 'I was just going.' He moved near the door. Sutro said sharply: 'Let's have the story first.'

Dalmas said: 'Sure.'

He moved lithely, without haste, and threw the door wide open. The gun jerked up in Sutro's hand. Dalmas said: 'Don't be a sap. You're not starting anything here and you know it.'

The two men stared at each other. After a moment or two Sutro put the gun back into his pocket and licked his thin lips. Dalmas said: 'Miss Dalton had a gun once that killed a man – recently. But she hasn't had it for a long time. That's all I wanted to know.'

Sutro nodded slowly. There was a peculiar expression in his eyes.

'Miss Dalton is a friend of my wife's. I wouldn't want her to be bothered,' he said coldly.

'That's right. You wouldn't,' Dalmas said. 'But a legitimate dick has a right to ask legitimate questions. I didn't break in here.'

Sutro eyed him slowly: 'Okay, but take it easy on my friends. I draw water in this town and I could hang a sign on you.'

Dalmas nodded. He went quietly out of the door and shut it. He listened a moment. There was no sound inside that he could hear. He shrugged and went on down the hall, down three steps and across a small lobby that had no switchboard. Outside the apartment house he looked along the street. It was an apartment-house district and there were cars parked up and down the street. He went towards the lights of the taxi that was waiting for him.

Joey, the red-haired driver, was standing on the edge of the kerb in front of his hack. He was smoking a cigarette, staring

across the street, apparently at a big, dark coupé that was parked
with its left side to the kerb. As Dalmas came up to him he
threw his cigarette away and came to meet him.

He spoke quickly: 'Listen, boss. I got a look at the guy in
that Cad—'

Pale flame broke in bitter streaks from above the door of the
coupé. A gun racketed between the buildings that faced each
other across the street. Joey fell against Dalmas. The coupé
jerked into sudden motion. Dalmas went down sidewise, on to
one knee, with the driver clinging to him. He tried to reach his
gun, couldn't make it. The coupé went around the corner with
a squeal of rubber, and Joey fell down Dalmas' side and rolled
over on his back on the sidewalk. He beat his hands up and
down on the cement and a hoarse, anguished sound came from
deep inside him.

Tyres screeched again, and Dalmas flung up to his feet, swept
his hand to his left armpit. He relaxed as a small car skidded to a
stop and Denny fell out of it, charged across the intervening
space towards him.

Dalmas bent over the driver. Light from the lanterns beside
the entrance to the apartment house showed blood on the front
of Joey's whipcord jacket, blood that was seeping out through
the material. Joey's eyes opened and shut like the eyes of a dying
bird.

Denny said: 'No use to follow that bus. Too fast.'

'Get to a phone and call an ambulance,' Dalmas said quickly.
'The kid's got a bellyful. . . . Then take a plant on the blonde.'

The big man hurried back to his car, jumped into it and tore
off around the corner. A window went open somewhere and a
man yelled down. Some cars stopped.

Dalmas bent down over Joey and muttered: 'Take it easy,
oldtimer. . . . Easy, boy . . . easy.'

7

The homicide lieutenant's name was Weinkassel. He had thin,
blond hair, icy blue eyes and a lot of pockmarks. He sat in a

swivel chair with his feet on the edge of a pulled-out drawer and a telephone scooped close to his elbow. The room smelled of dust and cigar butts.

A man named Lonergan, a bulky dick with grey hair and a grey moustache, stood near an open window, looking out of it morosely.

Weinkassel chewed on a match, stared at Dalmas, who was across the desk from him. He said: 'Better talk a bit. The hack driver can't. You've had luck in this town and you wouldn't want to run it into the ground.'

Lonergan said: 'He's hard. He won't talk.' He didn't turn around when he said it.

'A little less of your crap would go farther, Lonnie,' Weinkassel said in a dead voice.

Dalmas smiled faintly and rubbed the palm of his hand against the side of the desk. It made a squeaking sound.

'What would I talk about?' he asked. 'It was dark and I didn't get a flash of the man behind the gun. The car was a Cadillac coupé, without lights. I've told you this already, Lieutenant.'

'It don't listen,' Weinkassel grumbled. 'There's something screwy about it. You gotta have some kind of a hunch who it could be. It's a cinch the gun was for you.'

Dalmas said: 'Why? The hack driver was hit and I wasn't. Those lads get around a lot. One of them might be in wrong with some tough boys.'

'Like you,' Lonergan said. He went on staring out of the window.

Weinkassel frowned at Lonergan's back and said patiently: 'The car was outside while you was still inside. The hack driver was outside. If the guy with the gun had wanted him, he didn't have to wait for you to come out.'

Dalmas spread his hands and shrugged. 'You boys think I know who it was?'

'Not exactly. We think you could give us some names to check on, though. Who'd you go to see in them apartments?'

Dalmas didn't say anything for a moment. Lonergan turned away from the window, sat on the end of the desk and swung his legs. There was a cynical grin on his flat face.

'Come through, baby,' he said cheerfully.

Dalmas tilted his chair back and put his hands into his pockets. He stared at Weinkassel speculatively, ignored the grey-haired dick as though he didn't exist.

He said slowly: 'I was there on business for a client. You can't make me talk about that.'

Weinkassel shrugged and stared at him coldly. Then he took the chewed match out of his mouth, looked at the flattened end of it, tossed it away.

'I might have a hunch your business had something to do with the shootin',' he said grimly. 'That way the hush-hush would be out. Wouldn't it?'

'Maybe,' Dalmas said. 'If that's the way it's going to work out. But I ought to have a chance to talk to my client.'

Weinkassel said: 'Oke. You can have till the morning. Then you put your papers on the desk, see.'

Dalmas nodded and stood up. 'Fair enough, Lieutenant.'

'Hush-hush is all a shamus knows,' Lonergan said roughly.

Dalmas nodded to Weinkassel and went out of the office. He walked down a bleak corridor and up steps to the lobby floor. Outside the City Hall he went down a long flight of concrete steps and across Spring Street to where a blue Packard roadster, not very new, was parked. He got into it and drove around the corner, then through the Second Street tunnel, dropped over a block and drove out west. He watched in the mirror as he drove.

At Alvarado he went into a drugstore and called his hotel. The clerk gave him a number to call. He called it and heard Denny's heavy voice at the other end of the line. Denny said urgently: 'Where you been? I've got that broad out here at my place. She's drunk. Come on out and we'll get her to tell us what you want to know.'

Dalmas stared out through the glass of the phone booth

without seeing anything. After a pause he said slowly: 'The blonde? How come?'

'It's a story, boy. Come on out and I'll give it to you. Fourteen-fifty-four South Livesay. Know where that is?'

'I've got a map. I'll find it,' Dalmas said in the same tone.

Denny told him just how to find it, at some length. At the end of the explanation he said: 'Make it fast. She's asleep now, but she might wake up and start yellin' murder.'

Dalmas said: 'Where you live it probably wouldn't matter much. . . . I'll be right out, Denny.'

He hung up and went out to his car. He got a pint bottle of bourbon out of the car pocket and took a long drink. Then he started up and drove towards Fox Hills. Twice on the way he stopped and sat still in the car, thinking. But each time he went on again.

8

The road turned off Pico into a scattered subdivision that spread itself out over rolling hills between two golf courses. It followed the edge of one of the golf courses, separated from it by a high wire fence. There were bungalows here and there dotted about the slopes. After a while the road dipped into a hollow and there was a single bungalow in the hollow, right across the road from the golf course.

Dalmas drove past it and parked under a giant eucalyptus that etched deep shadow on the moonlit surface of the road. He got out and walked back, turned up a cement path to the bungalow. It was wide and low and had cottage windows across the front. Bushes grew halfway up the screens. There was faint light inside and the sound of a radio, turned low, came through the open windows.

A shadow moved across the screens and the front door came open. Dalmas went into a living-room built across the front of the house. One small bulb burned in a lamp and the luminous dial of the radio glowed. A little moonlight came into the room.

Denny had his coat off and his sleeves rolled up on his big arms.

He said: 'The broad's still asleep. I'll wake her up when I've told you how I got her here.'

Dalmas said: 'Sure you weren't tailed?'

'Not a chance.' Denny spread a big hand.

Dalmas sat down in a wicker chair in the corner, between the radio and the end of the line of windows. He put his hat on the floor, pulled out the bottle of bourbon and regarded it with a dissatisfied air.

'Buy us a real drink, Denny. I'm tired as hell. Didn't get any dinner.'

Denny said: 'I've got some Three-Star Martell. Be right up.'

He went out of the room and a light went on in the back part of the house. Dalmas put the bottle on the floor beside his hat and rubbed two fingers across his forehead. His head ached. After a little while the light went out in the back and Denny came back with two tall glasses.

The brandy tasted clean and hard. Denny sat down in another wicker chair. He looked very big and dark in the half-lit room. He began to talk slowly, in his gruff voice.

'It sounds goofy, but it worked. After the cops stopped milling around I parked in the alley and went in the back way. I knew which apartment the broad had but I hadn't seen her. I thought I'd make some kind of a stall and see how she was makin' out. I knocked on her door, but she wouldn't answer. I could hear her movin' around inside, and in a minute I could hear a telephone bein' dialled. I went back along the hall and tried the service door. It opened and I went in. It fastened with one of them screw bolts that get out of line and don't fasten when you think they do.'

Dalmas nodded, said: 'I get the idea, Denny.'

The big man drank out of his glass and rubbed the edge of it up and down on his lower lip. He went on.

'She was phoning a guy named Gayn Donner. Know him?'

'I've heard of him,' Dalmas said. 'So she has that kind of connexions.'

'She was callin' him by name and she sounded mad,' Denny said. 'That's how I knew. Donner has that place on Mariposa Canyon Drive – the Mariposa Club. You hear his band over the air – Hank Munn and his boys.'

Dalmas said: 'I've heard it, Denny.'

'Okay. When she hung up I went in on her. She looked snowed, weaved around funny, didn't seem to know much what was going on. I looked around and there was a photo of John Sutro, the councilman, in a desk there. I used that for a stall. I said that Sutro wanted her to duck out for a while and that I was one of his boys and she was to come along. She fell for it. Screwy. She wanted some liquor. I said I had some in the car. She got her little hat and coat.'

Dalmas said softly: 'It was that easy, huh?'

'Yeah,' Denny said. He finished his drink and put the glass somewhere. 'I bottle-fed her in the car to keep her quiet and we came out here. She went to sleep and that's that. What do you figure? Tough downtown?'

'Tough enough,' Dalmas said. 'I didn't fool the boys much.'

'Anything on the Walden kill?'

Dalmas shook his head slowly.

'I guess the Jap didn't get home yet, Denny.'

'Want to talk to the broad?'

The radio was playing a waltz. Dalmas listened to it for a moment before he answered. Then he said in a tired voice: 'I guess that's what I came out here for.'

Denny got up and went out of the room. There was the sound of a door opening and muffled voices.

Dalmas took his gun out from under his arm and put it down in the chair beside his leg.

The blonde staggered a little too much as she came in. She stared around, giggled, made vague motions with her long hands. She blinked at Dalmas, stood swaying a moment, then slid down into the chair Denny had been sitting in. The big man kept near her and leaned against a library table that stood by the inside wall.

She said drunkenly: 'My old pal the dick. Hey, hey, stranger! How about buyin' a lady a drink?'

Dalmas stared at her without expression. He said slowly: 'Got any new ideas about that gun? You know, the one we were talking about when Johnny Sutro crashed in.... The filed gun.... The gun that killed Derek Walden.'

Denny stiffened, then made a sudden motion towards his hip. Dalmas brought his Colt up and came to his feet with it. Denny looked at it and became still, relaxed. The girl had not moved at all, but the drunkenness dropped away from her like a dead leaf. Her face was suddenly tense and bitter.

Dalmas said evenly: 'Keep the hands in sight, Denny, and everything'll be jake.... Now suppose you two cheap crossers tell me what I'm here for.'

The big man said thickly: 'For gawd's sake! What's eatin' you? You scared me when you said "Walden" to the girl.'

Dalmas grinned. 'That's all right, Denny. Maybe she never heard of him. Let's get this ironed out in a hurry. I have an idea I'm here for trouble.'

'You're crazy as hell!' the big man snarled.

Dalmas moved the gun slightly. He put his back against the end wall of the room, leaned over and turned the radio off with his left hand. Then he spoke bitterly: 'You sold out, Denny. That's easy. You're too big for a tail and I've spotted you following me around half a dozen times lately. When you horned in on the deal tonight I was pretty sure.... And when you told me that funny story about how you got baby out here I was *damn* sure.... Hell's sake, do you think a guy that's stayed alive as long as I have would believe that one? Come on, Denny, be a sport and tell me who you're working for ... I might let you take a powder.... Who you working for? Donner? Sutro? Or somebody I don't know? And why the plant out here in the woods?'

The girl shot to her feet suddenly and sprang at him. He

threw her off with his free hand and she sprawled on the floor. She yelled: 'Get him, you big punk! Get him!'

Denny didn't move. 'Shut up, snow-bird!' Dalmas snapped. 'Nobody's getting anybody. This is just a talk between friends. Get up on your feet and stop throwing curves!'

The blonde stood up slowly.

Denny's face had a stony, immovable look in the dimness. His voice came with a dull rasp. He said: 'I sold out. It was lousy. Okay, that's that. I got fed up with watchin' a bunch of extra girls trying to pinch each other's lipstick. . . . You can take a plug at me if you feel like it.'

He still didn't move. Dalmas nodded slowly and said again: 'Who is it, Denny? Who you working for?'

Denny said: 'I don't know. I call a number, get orders, and report that way. I get dough in the mail. I tried to break the twist here, but no luck. . . . I don't think you're on the spot and I don't know a damn thing about that shootin' in the street.'

Dalmas stared at him. He said slowly: 'You wouldn't be stalling – to keep me here – would you, Denny?'

The big man raised his head slowly. The room suddenly seemed to get very still. A car had stopped outside. The faint throbbing of its motor died.

A red spotlight hit the top of the screens.

It was blinding. Dalmas slid down on one knee, shifted his position sidewise very quickly, silently. Denny's harsh voice in the silence said: 'Cops, for gawd's sake!'

The red light dissolved the wire mesh of the screens into a rosy glow, threw a great splash of vivid colour on the oiled finish of the inside wall. The girl made a choked sound and her face was a red mask for an instant before she sank down out of the fan of light. Dalmas looked into the light, his head low behind the sill of the end window. The leaves of the bushes were black spearpoints in the red glare.

Steps sounded on the walk.

A harsh voice rasped: 'Everybody out! Mitts in the air!'

There was a sound of movement inside the house. Dalmas

swung his gun – uselessly. A switch clicked and a porch light went on. For a moment, before they dodged back, two men in blue police uniforms showed up in the cone of the porch light. One of them held a submachine gun and the other had a long Luger with a special magazine fitted to it.

There was a grating sound. Denny was at the door, opening the peep panel. A gun came up in his hand and crashed.

Something heavy clattered on the cement and a man swayed forward into the light, swayed back again. His hands were against his middle. A stiff-visored cap fell down and rolled on the walk.

Dalmas hit the floor low down against the baseboard as the machine-gun cut loose. He ground his face into the wood of the floor. The girl screamed behind him.

The chopper raked the room swiftly from end to end and the air filled with plaster and splinters. A wall mirror crashed down. A sharp stench of powder fought with the sour smell of the plaster dust. This seemed to go on for a very long time. Something fell across Dalmas' legs. He kept his eyes shut and his face pressed against the floor.

The stuttering and crashing stopped. The rain of plaster inside the walls kept on. A voice yelled: 'How d'you like it, pals?'

Another voice far back snapped angrily: 'Come on – let's go!'

Steps sounded again, and a dragging sound. More steps. The motor of the car roared into life. A door slammed heavily. Tyres screeched on the gravel of the road and the song of the motor swelled and died swiftly.

Dalmas got up on his feet. His ears boomed and his nostrils were dry. He got his gun off the floor, unclipped a thin flash from an inside pocket, snapped it on. It probed weakly through the dusty air. The blonde lay on her back with her eyes wide open and her mouth twisted into a sort of grin. She was sobbing. Dalmas bent over her. There didn't seem to be a mark on her.

He went on down the room. He found his hat untouched beside a chair that had half the top shot off. The bottle of bourbon lay beside the hat. He picked them both up. The man with the chopper had raked the room waist-high, back and forth, without lowering it far enough. Dalmas went on farther, came to the door.

Denny was on his knees in front of the door. He was swaying backwards and forwards and holding one of his hands in the other. Blood dribbled between his thick fingers.

Dalmas got the door open and went out. There was a smear of blood and a litter of shells on the walk. There was nobody in sight. He stood there with the blood beating in his face, like little hammers. The skin around his nose prickled.

He drank some whisky out of the bottle and turned and went back into the house. Denny was up on his feet now. He had a handkerchief out and was tying it around his bloody hand. He looked dazed, drunk. He swayed on his feet. Dalmas put the beam of the flash on his face.

He said: 'Hurt much?'

'No. Clipped on the hand,' the big man said thickly. His fingers were clumsy on the handkerchief.

'The blonde's scared blind,' Dalmas said. 'It's your party, boy. Nice pals you have. They meant to get all three of us. You rattled them when you took a pot out of the peephole. I guess I owe you something for that, Denny. . . . The gunner wasn't so good.'

Denny said: 'Where you goin'?'

'Where d'you think?'

Denny looked at him. 'Sutro's your man,' he said slowly. 'I'm through – washed up. They can all go to hell.'

Dalmas went through the door again, down the path to the roadway. He got into his car and drove away without lights. When he had turned corners and gone some distance he switched the lights on and got out and dusted himself off.

9

Black and silver curtains opened in an inverted V against a haze of cigarette and cigar smoke. The brasses of the dance band shot brief flashes of colour through the haze. There was a smell of food and liquor and perfume and face powder. The dance floor was an empty splash of amber light and looked slightly larger than a screen star's bath mat.

Then the band started up and the lights went down, and a headwaiter came up the carpeted steps tapping a gold pencil against the satin stripe of his trousers. He had narrow, lifeless eyes and blond-white hair sleeked back off a bony forehead.

Dalmas said: 'I'd like to see Mister Donner.'

The headwaiter tapped his teeth with his gold pencil. 'I'm afraid he's busy. What name?'

'Dalmas. Tell him I'm a special friend of Johnny Sutro's.'

The headwaiter said: 'I'll try.'

He went across to a panel that had a row of buttons on it and a small one-piece phone. He took it off the hook and put it to his ear, staring at Dalmas across the cup with the impersonal stare of a stuffed animal.

Dalmas said: 'I'll be in the lobby.'

He went back through the curtains and prowled over to the men's room. Inside he got out the bottle of bourbon and drank what was left of it, tilting his head back and standing splay-legged in the middle of the tiled floor. A wizened negro in a white jacket fluttered at him, said anxiously: 'No drinkin' in here, boss.'

Dalmas threw the empty bottle into a receptacle for towels. He took a clean towel off the glass shelf, wiped his lips with it, put a dime down on the edge of the basin and went out.

There was a space between an inner and outer door. He leaned against the outer door and took a small automatic about four inches long out of his vest pocket. He held it with three fingers against the inside of his hat and went on out, swinging the hat gently beside his body.

After a while a tall Filipino with silky black hair came into the lobby and looked around. Dalmas went towards him. The headwaiter looked out through the curtains and nodded at the Filipino.

The Filipino spoke to Dalmas: 'This way, boss.'

They went down a long, quiet corridor. The sound of the dance band died away behind them. Some deserted green-topped tables showed through an open door. The corridor turned into another that was at right angles, and at the end of this one some light came out through a doorway.

The Filipino paused in midstride and made a graceful, complicated movement, at the end of which he had a big, black automatic in his hand. He prodded it politely into Dalmas' ribs.

'Got to frisk you, boss. House rules.'

Dalmas stood still and held his arms out from his sides. The Filipino took Dalmas' Colt away from him and dropped it into his pocket. He patted the rest of Dalmas' pockets, stepped back and holstered his own cannon.

Dalmas lowered his arms and let his hat fall on the floor and the little automatic that had been inside the hat peered neatly at the Filipino's belly. The Filipino looked down at it with a shocked grin.

Dalmas said: 'That was fun, spig. Let me do it.'

He put his Colt back where it belonged, took the big automatic from under the Filipino's arm, slipped the magazine out of it and ejected the shell that was in the chamber. He gave the empty gun back to the Filipino.

'You can still use it for a cosh. If you stay in front of me, your boss don't have to know that's all it's good for.'

The Filipino licked his lips. Dalmas felt him for another gun, and they went on along the corridor, went in at the door that was partly open. The Filipino went first.

It was a big room with walls panelled in diagonal strips of wood. A yellow Chinese rug on the floor, plenty of good furniture, countersunk doors that told of soundproofing, and no windows. There were several gilt gratings high up and a built-in ventilator fan made a faint, soothing murmur. Four men were in the room. Nobody said anything.

Dalmas sat down on a leather divan and stared at Ricchio, the smooth boy who had walked him out of Walden's apartment. Ricchio was tied to a high-backed chair. His arms were pulled around behind it and fastened together at the wrists. His eyes were mad and his face was a welter of blood and bruises. He had been pistol whipped. The sandy-haired man, Noddy, who had been with him at the Kilmarnock sat on a sort of stool in the corner, smoking.

John Sutro was rocking slowly in a red leather rocker, staring down at the floor. He did not look up when Dalmas came into the room.

The fourth man sat behind a desk that looked as if it had cost a lot of money. He had soft brown hair parted in the middle and brushed back and down; thin lips and reddish-brown eyes that had hot lights in them. He watched Dalmas while he sat down and looked around. Then he spoke, glancing at Ricchio.

'The punk got a little out of hand. We've been telling him about it. I guess you're not sorry.'

Dalmas laughed shortly, without mirth. 'All right as far as it goes, Donner. How about the other one? I don't see any marks on him.'

'Noddy's all right. He worked under orders,' Donner said evenly. He picked up a long-handled file and began to file one of his nails. 'You and I have things to talk about. That's why you got in here. You look all right to me – if you don't try to cover too much ground with your private-dick racket.'

Dalmas' eyes widened a little. He said: 'I'm listening, Donner.'

Sutro lifted his eyes and stared at the back of Donner's head. Donner went on talking in a smooth, indifferent voice.

'I know all about the play at Derek Walden's place and I know about the shooting on Kenmore. If I'd thought Ricchio would go that crazy, I'd have stopped him before. As it is, I figure it's up to me to straighten things out. . . . And when we get through here Mister Ricchio will go downtown and speak his piece.

'Here's how it happened. Ricchio used to work for Walden when the Hollywood crowd went in for bodyguards. Walden bought his liquor in Ensenada – still does, for all I know – and brought it in himself. Nobody bothered him. Ricchio saw a chance to bring in some white goods under good cover. Walden caught him at it. He didn't want a scandal, so he just showed Ricchio the gate. Ricchio took advantage of that by trying to shake Walden down, on the theory that he wasn't clean enough to stand the working-over the Feds would give him. Walden didn't shake fast enough to suit Ricchio, so he went hog-wild and decided on a strong-arm play. You and your driver messed it up and Ricchio went gunning for you.'

Donner put down his file and smiled. Dalmas shrugged and glanced at the Filipino, who was standing by the wall, at the end of the divan.

Dalmas said: 'I don't have your organization, Donner, but I get around. I think that's a smooth story and it would have got by – with a little co-operation downtown. But it won't fit the facts as they are now.'

Donner raised his eyebrows. Sutro began to swing the tip of his polished shoe up and down in front of his knee.

Dalmas said: 'How does Mister Sutro fit into all this?'

Sutro stared at him and stopped rocking. He made a swift, impatient movement. Donner smiled. 'He's a friend of Walden's. Walden talked to him a little and Sutro knows Ricchio worked for me. But being a councilman he didn't want to tell Walden everything he knew.'

Dalmas said grimly: 'I'll tell you what's wrong with your story, Donner. There's not enough fear in it. Walden was too scared to help me even when I was working for him. . . . And this afternoon somebody was so scared of him that he got shot.'

Donner leaned forward and his eyes got small and tight. His hands balled into fists on the desk before him.

'Walden is – dead?' he almost whispered.

Dalmas nodded. 'Shot in the right temple . . . with a .32. It looks like suicide. It isn't.'

Sutro put his hand up quickly and covered his face. The sandy-haired man got rigid on his stool in the corner.

Dalmas said: 'Want to hear a good honest guess, Donner? . . . We'll call it a guess . . . Walden was in the dope-smuggling racket himself – and not all by his lonesome. But after Repeal he wanted to quit. The coastguards wouldn't have to spend so much time watching liquor ships, and dope-smuggling up the coast wasn't going to be gravy any more. And Walden got sweet on a gal that had good eyes and could add up to ten. So he wanted to walk out on the dope racket.'

Donner moistened his lips and said: 'What dope racket?'

Dalmas eyed him. 'You wouldn't know about anything like that, would you, Donner? Hell, no, that's something for the bad boys to play with. And the bad boys didn't like the idea of Walden quitting that way. He was drinking too much – and he might start to broadcast to his girl friend. They wanted him to quit the way he did – on the receiving end of a gun.'

Donner turned his head slowly and stared at the bound man on the high-backed chair. He said very softly: 'Ricchio.'

Then he got up and walked around his desk. Sutro took his hand down from his face and watched with his lips shaking.

Donner stood in front of Ricchio. He put his hand out against Ricchio's head and jarred it back against the chair. Ricchio moaned. Donner smiled down at him.

'I must be slowing up. *You* killed Walden, you bastard! You went back and croaked him. You forgot to tell us about that part, baby.'

Ricchio opened his mouth and spat a stream of blood against Donner's hand and wrist. Donner's face twitched and he stepped back and away, holding the hand straight out in front of him. He took out a handkerchief and wiped it off carefully, dropped the handkerchief on the floor.

'Lend me your gun, Noddy,' he said quietly, going towards the sandy-haired man.

Sutro jerked and his mouth fell open. His eyes looked sick. The tall Filipino flicked his empty automatic into his hand as if he had forgotten it was empty. Noddy took a blunt revolver from under his right arm, held it out to Donner.

Donner took it from him and went back to Ricchio. He raised the gun.

Dalmas said: 'Ricchio didn't kill Walden.'

The Filipino took a quick step forward and slashed at him with his big automatic. The gun hit Dalmas on the point of the shoulder, and a wave of pain billowed down his arm. He rolled away and snapped his Colt into his hand. The Filipino swung at him again, missed.

Dalmas slid to his feet, side-stepped, and laid the barrel of the Colt along the side of the Filipino's head, with all his strength. The Filipino grunted, sat down on the floor, and the whites showed all around his eyes. He fell over slowly, clawing at the divan.

There was no expression on Donner's face and he held his blunt revolver perfectly still. His long upper lip was beaded with sweat.

Dalmas said: 'Ricchio didn't kill Walden. Walden was killed with a filed gun and the gun was planted in his hand. Ricchio wouldn't go within a block of a filed gun.'

Sutro's face was ghastly. The sandy-haired man had got down off his stool and stood with his right hand swinging at his side.

'Tell me more,' Donner said evenly.

'The filed gun traces to a broad named Helen Dalton or Burwand,' Dalmas said. 'It was her gun. She told me that she hocked it long ago. I didn't believe her. She's a good friend of Sutro's and Sutro was so bothered by my going to see her that he pulled a gat on me himself. Why do you suppose Sutro was bothered, Donner, and how do you suppose he knew I was likely to go see the broad?'

Donner said: 'Go ahead and tell me.' He looked at Sutro very quietly.

Dalmas took a step closer to Donner and held his Colt down at his side, not threateningly.

'I'll tell you how and why. I've been tailed ever since I started to work for Walden – tailed by a clumsy ox of a studio dick I could spot a mile off. He was bought, Donner. The guy that killed Walden bought him. He figured the studio dick had a chance to get next to me, and I let him do just that – to give him rope and spot his game. His boss was Sutro. Sutro killed Walden – with his own hand. It was that kind of a job. An amateur job – a smart-aleck kill. The thing that made it smart was the thing that gave it away – the suicide plant, with a filed gun that the killer thought couldn't be traced because he didn't know most guns have numbers inside.'

Donner swung the blunt revolver until it pointed midway between the sandy-haired man and Sutro. He didn't say anything. His eyes were thoughtful and interested.

Dalmas shifted his weight a little, on to the balls of his feet. The Filipino on the floor put a hand along the divan and his nails scratched on the leather.

'There's more of it, Donner, but what the hell! Sutro was Walden's pal, and he could get close to him, close enough to stick a gun to his head and let go. A shot wouldn't be heard on the penthouse floor of the Kilmarnock, one little shot from a thirty-two. So Sutro put the gun in Walden's hand and went on his way. But he forgot that Walden was left-handed and he didn't know the gun could be traced. When it was – and his bought man wised him up – and I tapped the girl – he hired himself a chopper squad and angled all three of us out to a house in Palms to button our mouths for good. . . . Only the chopper squad, like everything else in this play, didn't do its stuff so good.'

Donner nodded slowly. He looked at a spot in the middle of Sutro's stomach and lined his gun on it.

'Tell us about it, Johnny,' he said softly. 'Tell us how you got clever in your old age—'

The sandy-haired man moved suddenly. He dodged down

behind the desk and as he went down his right hand swept for his other gun. It roared from behind the desk. The bullet came through the knee-hole and pinged into the wall with a sound of striking metal behind the panelling.

Dalmas jerked his Colt and fired twice into the desk. A few splinters flew. The sandy-haired man yelled behind the desk and came up fast with his gun flaming in his hand. Donner staggered. His gun spoke twice, very quickly. The sandy-haired man yelled again, and blood jumped straight out from one of his cheeks. He went down behind the desk and stayed quiet.

Donner backed until he touched the wall. Sutro stood up and put his hands in front of his stomach and tried to scream.

Donner said: 'Okay, Johnny. Your turn.'

Then Donner coughed suddenly and slid down the wall with a dry rustle of cloth. He bent forward and dropped his gun and put his hands on the floor and went on coughing. His face got grey.

Sutro stood rigid, his hands in front of his stomach and bent back at the wrists, the fingers curved clawlike. There was no light behind his eyes. They were dead eyes. After a moment his knees buckled and he fell down on the floor on his back.

Donner went on coughing quietly.

Dalmas crossed swiftly to the door of the room, listened at it, opened it and looked out. He shut it again quickly.

'Soundproof – and how!' he muttered.

He went back to the desk and lifted the telephone off its prongs. He put his Colt down and dialled, waited, said into the phone: 'Captain Cathcart. . . . Got to talk to him. . . . Sure, it's important . . . very important.'

He waited, drumming on the desk, staring hard-eyed around the room. He jerked a little as a sleepy voice came over the wire.

'Dalmas, Chief. I'm at the Casa Mariposa, in Gayn Donner's private office. There's been a little trouble, but nobody hurt bad. . . . I've got Derek Walden's killer for you . . . Johnny Sutro did it. . . . Yeah, the councilman. . . . Make it fast,

Chief . . . I wouldn't want to get in a fight with the help, you know. . . .'

He hung up and picked his Colt off the top of the desk, held it on the flat of his hand and stared across at Sutro.

'Get up off the floor, Johnny,' he said wearily. 'Get up and tell a poor dumb dick how to cover this one up – smart guy!'

10

The light above the big oak table at Headquarters was too bright. Dalmas ran a finger along the wood, looked at it, wiped it off on his sleeve. He cupped his chin in his lean hands and stared at the wall above the roll-top desk that was beyond the table. He was alone in the room.

The loudspeaker on the wall droned: 'Calling Car 71W in 72's district . . . at Third and Berendo . . . at the drugstore . . . meet a man . . .'

The door opened and Captain Cathcart came in, shut the door carefully behind him. He was a big, battered man with a wide, moist face, a stained moustache, gnarled hands.

He sat down between the oak table and the roll-top desk and fingered a cold pipe that lay in the ashtray.

Dalmas raised his head from between his hands. Cathcart said: 'Sutro's dead.'

Dalmas stared, said nothing.

'His wife did it. He wanted to stop by his house a minute. The boys watched him good but they didn't watch her. She slipped him the dose before they could move.'

Cathcart opened and shut his mouth twice. He had strong, dirty teeth.

'She never said a damn word. Brought a little gun around from behind her and fed him three slugs. One, two, three. Win, place, show. Just like that. Then she turned the gun around in her hand as nice as you could think of and handed it to the boys. . . . What in hell she do that for?'

Dalmas said: 'Get a confession?'

Cathcart stared at him and put the cold pipe in his mouth.

He sucked on it noisily. 'From him? Yeah – not on paper, though. . . . What you suppose she done that for?'

'She knew about the blonde,' Dalmas said. 'She thought it was her last chance. Maybe she knew about his rackets.'

The captain nodded slowly. 'Sure,' he said. 'That's it. She figured it was her last chance. And why shouldn't she bop the bastard? If the D.A.'s smart, he'll let her take a manslaughter plea. That'd be about fifteen months at Tehachapi. A rest cure.'

Dalmas moved in his chair. He frowned.

Cathcart went on: 'It's a break for all of us. No dirt your way, no dirt on the administration. If she hadn't done it, it would have been a kick in the pants all around. She ought to get a pension.'

'She ought to get a contract from Eclipse Films,' Dalmas said. 'When I got to Sutro I figured I was licked on the publicity angle. I might have gunned Sutro myself – if he hadn't been so yellow – and if he hadn't been a councilman.'

'Nix on that, baby. Leave that stuff to the law,' Cathcart growled. 'Here's how it looks. I don't figure we can get Walden on the book as a suicide. The filed gun is against it and we got to wait for the autopsy and the gun-shark's report. And a paraffin test of the hand ought to show he didn't fire the gun at all. On the other hand, the case is closed on Sutro and what has to come out ought not to hurt too bad. Am I right?'

Dalmas took out a cigarette and rolled it between his fingers. He lit it slowly and waved the match until it went out.

'Walden was no lily,' he said. 'It's the dope angle that would raise hell – but that's cold. I guess we're jake, except for a few loose ends.'

'Hell with the loose ends,' Cathcart grinned. 'Nobody's getting away with any fix that I can see. That sidekick of yours, Denny, will fade in a hurry, and if I ever get my paws on the Dalton frail, I'll send her to Mendocino for the cure. We might get something on Donner – after the hospital gets through with him. We've got to put the rap on those hoods, for the stick-up and the taxi driver, whichever of 'em did that, but they won't talk. They still got a future to think about, and the taxi driver ain't so bad hurt. That leaves the chopper squad.' Cathcart yawned. 'Those boys must be from 'Frisco. We don't run to choppers around here much.'

Dalmas sagged in his chair. 'You wouldn't have a drink, would you, Chief?' he said dully.

Cathcart stared at him. 'There's just one thing,' he said grimly. 'I want you to stay told about that. It was okay for you to break that gun – if you didn't spoil the prints. And I guess it was okay for you not to tell me, seein' the jam you were in. But I'll be damned if it's okay for you to beat our time by chisellin' on our own records.'

Dalmas smiled thoughtfully at him. 'You're right all the way, Chief,' he said humbly. 'It was the job – and that's all a guy can say.'

Cathcart rubbed his cheeks vigorously. His frown went away and he grinned. Then he bent over and pulled out a drawer and brought up a quart bottle of rye. He put it on the desk and pressed a buzzer. A very large uniformed torso came part way into the room.

'Hey, Tiny!' Cathcart boomed. 'Loan me that corkscrew you swiped out of my desk.' The torso disappeared and came back.

'What'll we drink to?' the captain asked a couple of minutes later.

Dalmas said: 'Let's just drink.'

Pick-Up on Noon Street

I

The man and the girl walked slowly, close together, past a dim stencil sign that said: SURPRISE HOTEL. The man wore a purple suit, a panama hat over his shiny, slicked-down hair. He walked splay-footed, soundlessly.

The girl wore a green hat and a short skirt and sheer stockings, four-and-a-half-inch French heels. She smelled of Midnight Narcissus.

At the corner the man leaned close, said something in the girl's ear. She jerked away from him, giggled.

'You gotta buy liquor if you take *me* home, Smiler.'

'Next time, baby. I'm fresh outa dough.'

The girl's voice got hard. 'Then I tells you good-bye in the next block, handsome.'

'Like hell, baby,' the man answered.

The arc at the intersection threw light on them. They walked across the street far apart. At the other side the man caught the girl's arm. She twisted away from him.

'Listen, you cheap grifter!' she shrilled. 'Keep your paws down, see! Tinhorns are dust to me. Dangle!'

'How much liquor you gotta have, baby?'

'Plenty.'

'Me bein' on the nut, where do I collect it?'

'You got hands, ain't you?' the girl sneered. Her voice dropped the shrillness. She leaned close to him again. 'Maybe you got a gun, big boy. Got a gun?'

'Yeah. And no shells for it.'

'The goldbricks over on Central don't know that.'

'Don't be that way,' the man in the purple suit snarled. Then he snapped his fingers and stiffened. 'Wait a minute. I got me an idea.'

He stopped and looked back along the street towards the dim stencil hotel sign. The girl slapped a glove across his chin caressingly. The glove smelled to him of the perfume, Midnight Narcissus.

The man snapped his fingers again, grinned widely in the dim light. 'If that drunk is still holed up in Doc's place – I collect. Wait for me, huh?'

'Maybe, at home. If you ain't gone too long.'

'Where's home, baby?'

The girl stared at him. A half-smile moved along her full lips, died at the corners of them. The breeze picked a sheet of newspaper out of the gutter and tossed it against the man's leg. He kicked at it savagely.

'Calliope Apartments, 4-B, 246 East 48. How soon you be there?'

The man stepped very close to her, reached back and tapped his hip. His voice was low, chilling.

'You wait for me, baby.'

She caught her breath, nodded. 'Okay, handsome. I'll wait.'

The man went back along the cracked sidewalk, across the intersection, along to where the stencil sign hung out over the street. He went through a glass door into a narrow lobby with a row of brown wooden chairs pushed against the plaster wall. There was just space to walk past them to the desk. A bald-headed coloured man lounged behind the desk, fingering a large green pin in his tie.

The negro in the purple suit leaned across the counter and his teeth flashed in a quick, hard smile. He was very young, with a thin, sharp jaw; a narrow bony forehead, the flat brilliant eyes of the gangster. He said softly: 'That pug with the husky voice still here? The guy that banked the crap game last night.'

The bald-headed clerk looked at the flies on the ceiling fixture. 'Didn't see him go out, Smiler.'

'Ain't what I asked you, Doc.'

'Yeah. He still here.'

'Still drunk?'

'Guess so. Hasn't been out.'

'Three-forty-nine, ain't it?'

'You been there, ain't you? What you wanta know for?'

'He cleaned me down to my lucky piece. I gotta make a touch.'

The bald-headed man looked nervous. The Smiler stared softly at the green stone in the man's tie-pin.

'Get rolling, Smiler. Nobody gets bent around here. We ain't no Central Avenue flop.'

The Smiler said very softly: 'He's my pal, Doc. He'll lend me twenty. You touch half.'

He put his hand out palm up. The clerk stared at the hand for a long moment. Then he nodded sourly, went behind a ground-glass screen, came back slowly, looking towards the street door.

His hand went out and hovered over the palm. The palm closed over a pass-key, dropped inside the cheap purple suit.

The sudden flashing grin on the Smiler's face had an icy edge to it.

'Careful, Doc – while I'm up above.'

The clerk said: 'Step on it. Some of the customers get home early.' He glanced at the green electric clock on the wall. It was seven-fifteen. 'And the walls ain't any too thick,' he added.

The thin youth gave him another flashing grin, nodded, went delicately back along the lobby to the shadowy staircase. There was no elevator in the Surprise Hotel.

At one minute past seven Pete Anglich, narcotic squad undercover man, rolled over on the hard bed and looked at the cheap strap watch on his left wrist. There were heavy shadows under his eyes, a thick dark stubble on his broad chin. He swung his bare feet to the floor and stood up in cheap cotton pyjamas, flexed his muscles, stretched, bent over stiff-kneed and touched the floor in front of his toes with a grunt.

He walked across to a chipped bureau, drank from a quart bottle of cheap rye whisky, grimaced, pushed the cork into the neck of the bottle, and rammed it down with the heel of his hand.

'Boy, have I got a hangover,' he grumbled huskily.

He stared at his face in the bureau mirror, at the stubble on his chin, the thick white scar on his throat close to the windpipe. His voice was husky because the bullet that had made the scar had done something to his vocal cords. It was a smooth huskiness, like the voice of a blues singer.

He stripped his pyjamas off and stood naked in the middle of the room, his toes fumbling the rough edge of a big rip in the carpet. His body was very broad, and that made him look a little shorter than he was. His shoulders sloped, his nose was a little thick, the skin over his cheekbones looked like leather. He had short, curly, black hair, utterly steady eyes, the small set mouth of a quick thinker.

He went into a dim, dirty bathroom, stepped into the tub and turned the shower on. The water was warmish, but not hot. He stood under it and soaped himself, rubbed his whole body over, kneaded his muscles, rinsed off.

He jerked a dirty towel off the rack and started to rub a glow into his skin.

A faint noise behind the loosely closed bathroom door stopped him. He held his breath, listened, heard the noise again, a creak of boarding, a click, a rustle of cloth. Pete Anglich reached for the door and pulled it open slowly.

The negro in the purple suit and panama hat stood beside the bureau, with Pete Anglich's coat in his hand. On the bureau in front of him were two guns. One of them was Pete Anglich's old worn Colt. The room door was shut and a key with a tag lay on the carpet near it, as though it had fallen out of the door, or been pushed out from the other side.

The Smiler let the coat fall to the floor and held a wallet in his left hand. His right hand lifted the Colt. He grinned.

'Okay, white boy. Just go on dryin' yourself off after your shower,' he said.

Pete Anglich towelled himself. He rubbed himself dry, stood naked with the wet towel in his left hand.

The Smiler had the billfold empty on the bureau, was counting the money with his left hand. His right still clutched the Colt.

'Eighty-seven bucks. Nice money. Some of it's mine from the crap game, but I'm lifting it all, pal. Take it easy. I'm friends with the management here.'

'Gimme a break, Smiler,' Pete Anglich said hoarsely. 'That's every dollar I got in the world. Leave a few bucks, huh?' He made his voice thick, coarse, heavy as though with liquor.

The Smiler gleamed his teeth, shook his narrow head. 'Can't do it, pal. Got me a date and I need the kale.'

Pete Anglich took a loose step forward and stopped, grinning sheepishly. The muzzle of his own gun had jerked at him.

The Smiler sidled over to the bottle of rye and lifted it.

'I can use this, too. My baby's got a throat for liquor. Sure has. What's in your pants is yours, pal. Fair enough?'

Pete Anglich jumped sideways, about four feet. The Smiler's face convulsed. The gun jerked around and the bottle of rye slid out of his left hand, slammed down on his foot. He yelped, kicked out savagely, and his toe caught in the torn place in the carpet.

Pete Anglich flipped the wet end of the bathtowel straight at the Smiler's eyes.

The Smiler reeled and yelled with pain. Then Pete Anglich held the Smiler's gun wrist in his hard left hand. He twisted up, around. His hand started to slide down over the Smiler's hand, over the gun. The gun turned inward and touched the Smiler's side.

A hard knee kicked viciously at Pete Anglich's abdomen. He gagged, and his finger tightened convulsively on the Smiler's trigger finger.

The shot was dull, muffled against the purple cloth of the suit. The Smiler's eyes rolled whitely and his narrow jaw fell slack.

Pete Anglich let him down on the floor and stood panting, bent over, his face greenish. He groped for the fallen bottle of rye, got the cork out, got some of the fiery liquid down his throat.

The greenish look went away from his face. His breathing slowed. He wiped sweat off his forehead with the back of his hand.

He felt the Smiler's pulse. The Smiler didn't have any pulse. He was dead. Pete Anglich loosened the gun from his hand, went over to the door and glanced out into the hallway. Empty. There was a pass-key in the outside of the lock. He removed it, locked the door from the inside.

He put his underclothes and socks and shoes on, his worn blue serge suit, knotted a black tie around the crumpled shirt collar, went back to the dead man and took a roll of bills from his pocket. He packed a few odds and ends of clothes and toilet articles in a cheap fibre suitcase, stood it by the door.

He pushed a torn scrap of sheet through his revolver barrel with a pencil, replaced the used cartridge, crushed the empty shell with his heel on the bathroom floor and then flushed it down the toilet.

He locked the door from the outside and walked down the stairs to the lobby.

The bald-headed clerk's eyes jumped at him, then dropped. The skin of his face turned grey. Pete Anglich leaned on the counter and opened his hand to let two keys tinkle on the scarred wood. The clerk stared at the keys, shuddered.

Pete Anglich said in his slow, husky voice: 'Hear any funny noises?'

The clerk shook his head, gulped.

'Creep joint, eh?' Pete Anglich said.

The clerk moved his head painfully, twisted his neck in his collar. His bald head winked darkly under the ceiling light.

'Too bad,' Pete Anglich said. 'What name did I register under last night?'

'You ain't registered,' the clerk whispered.

'Maybe I wasn't here even,' Pete Anglich said softly.

'Never saw you before, mister.'

'You're not seeing me now. You never will see me – to know me – will you, Doc?'

The clerk moved his neck and tried to smile.

Pete Anglich drew his wallet out and shook three dollar bills from it.

'I'm a guy that likes to pay his way,' he said slowly. 'This pays for Room 349 – till 'way in the morning, kind of late. The lad you gave the pass-key to looks like a heavy sleeper.' He paused, steadied his cool eyes on the clerk's face, added thoughtfully: 'Unless, of course, he's got friends who would like to move him out.'

Bubbles showed on the clerk's lips. He stuttered: 'He ain't – ain't—'

'Yeah,' Pete Anglich said. 'What would you expect?'

He went across to the street door, carrying his suitcase, stepped out under the stencil sign, stood a moment looking towards the hard white glare of Central Avenue.

Then he walked the other way. The street was very dark, very quiet. There were four blocks of frame houses before he came to Noon Street. It was all a negro quarter.

He met only one person on the way, a brown girl in a green hat, very sheer stockings, and four-and-a-half-inch heels, who smoked a cigarette under a dusty palm tree and stared back towards the Surprise Hotel.

2

The lunch wagon was an old buffet car without wheels, set end to the street in a space between a machine shop and a rooming house. The name BELLA DONNA was lettered in faded gold on the sides. Pete Anglich went up the two iron steps at the end, into a smell of fry grease.

The negro cook's fat white back was to him. At the far end of the low counter a white girl in a cheap brown felt hat and a shabby polo coat with a high turned-up collar was sipping coffee, her cheek propped in her left hand. There was nobody else in the car.

Pete Anglich put his suitcase down and sat on a stool near the door, saying: 'Hi, Mopsy!'

The fat cook turned a shiny black face over his white shoulder. The face split in a grin. A thick bluish tongue came out and wiggled between the cook's thick lips.

'How's a boy? W'at you eat?'

'Scramble two light, coffee, toast, no spuds.'

'Dat ain't no food for a he-guy,' Mopsy complained.

'I been drunk,' Pete Anglich said.

The girl at the end of the counter looked at him sharply, looked at the cheap alarm clock on the shelf, at the watch on her gloved wrist. She drooped, stared into her coffee cup again.

The fat cook broke eggs into a pan, added milk, stirred them around. 'You want a shot, boy?'

Pete Anglich shook his head.

'I'm driving the wagon, Mopsy.'

The cook grinned. He reached a brown bottle from under the counter, and poured a big drink into a water glass, set the glass down beside Pete Anglich.

Pete Anglich reached suddenly for the glass, jerked it to his lips, drank the liquor down.

'Guess I'll drive the wagon some other time.' He put the glass down empty.

The girl stood up, came along the stools, put a dime on the counter. The fat cook punched his cash register, put down a nickel change. Pete Anglich stared casually at the girl. A shabby, innocent-eyed girl, brown hair curling on her neck, eyebrows plucked clean as a bone and startled arches painted above the place where they had been.

'Not lost, are you, lady?' he asked in his softly husky voice.

The girl had fumbled her bag open to put the nickel away. She started violently, stepped back and dropped the bag. It spilled its contents on the floor. She stared down at it, wide-eyed.

Pete Anglich went down on one knee and pushed things into the bag. A cheap nickel compact, cigarettes, a purple match-folder lettered in gold: JUGGERNAUT CLUB. Two coloured handkerchiefs, a crumpled dollar bill and some silver and pennies.

He stood up with the closed bag in his hand, held it out to the girl.

'Sorry,' he said softly. 'I guess I startled you.'

Her breath made a rushing sound. She caught the bag out of his hand, ran out of the car, and was gone.

The fat cook looked after her. 'That doll don't belong in Tough Town,' he said slowly.

He dished up the eggs and toast, poured coffee in a thick cup, put them down in front of Pete Anglich.

Pete Anglich touched the food, said absently: 'Alone, and matches from the Juggernaut. Trimmer Waltz's spot. You know what happens to girls like that when he gets hold of them.'

The cook licked his lips, reached under the counter for the whisky bottle. He poured himself a drink, added about the same amount of water to the bottle, put it back under the counter.

'I ain't never been a tough guy, and don' want to start,' he said slowly. 'But I'se all tired of white boys like dat guy. Some day he gonna get cut.'

Pete Anglich kicked his suitcase.

'Yeah. Keep the case for me, Mopsy.'

He went out.

Two or three cars flicked by in the crisp fall night, but the sidewalks were dark and empty. A coloured night-watchman moved slowly along the street, trying the doors of a small row of dingy stores. There were frame houses across the street, and a couple of them were noisy.

Pete Anglich went on past the intersection. Three blocks from the lunch wagon he saw the girl again.

She was pressed against a wall, motionless. A little beyond her, dim yellow light came from the stairway of a walk-up apartment house. Beyond that a small parking lot with billboards across most of its front. Faint light from somewhere touched her hat, her shabby polo coat with the turned-up collar, one side of her face. He knew it was the same girl.

He stepped into a doorway, watched her. Light flashed on her upraised arm, on something bright, a wrist watch. Somewhere not far off a clock struck eight slow, pealing notes.

Lights stabbed into the street from the corner behind. A big car swung slowly into view and, as it swung, its headlights dimmed. It crept along the block, a dark shininess of glass and polished paint.

Pete Anglich grinned sharply in his doorway. A custombuilt Duesenberg, six blocks from Central Avenue! He stiffened at the sharp sound of running steps, clicking high heels.

The girl was running towards him along the sidewalk. The car was not near enough for its dimmed lights to pick her up. Pete Anglich stepped out of the doorway, grabbed her arm, dragged her back into the doorway. A gun snaked from under his coat.

The girl panted at his side.

The Duesenberg passed the doorway slowly. No shots came from it. The uniformed driver didn't slow down.

'I can't do it. I'm scared,' the girl gasped in Pete Anglich's ear. Then she broke away from him and ran farther along the sidewalk, away from the car.

Pete Anglich looked after the Duesenberg. It was opposite the row of billboards that screened the parking lot. It was barely crawling now. Something sailed from its left front window, fell with a dry slap on the sidewalk. The car picked up speed soundlessly, purred off into the darkness. A block away its headlights flashed up full again.

Nothing moved. The thing that had been thrown out of the car lay on the inner edge of the sidewalk, almost under one of the billboards.

Then the girl was coming back again, a step at a time, haltingly. Pete Anglich watched her come, without moving.

When she was level with him he said softly: 'What's the racket? Could a fellow help?'

She spun around with a choked sound, as though she had forgotten all about him. Her head moved in the darkness at his side. There was a swift shine as her eyes moved. There was a pale flicker across her chin. Her voice was low, hurried, scared.

'You're the man from the lunch wagon. I saw you.'

'Open up. What is it – a pay-off?'

Her head moved again in the darkness at his side, up and down.

'What's in the package?' Pete Anglich growled. 'Money?'

Her words came in a rush. 'Would you get it for me? Oh, would you, please? I'd be so grateful. I'd— '

He laughed. His laugh had a low growling sound. 'Get it for *you*, baby? I use money in my business, too. Come on, what's the racket? Spill.'

She jerked away from him, but he didn't let go of her arm. He slid the gun out of sight under his coat, held her with both hands. Her voice sobbed as she whispered: 'He'll kill me if I don't get it.'

Very sharply, coldly, Pete Anglich said, 'Who will? Trimmer Waltz?'

She started violently, almost tore out of his grasp. Not quite. Steps shuffled on the sidewalk. Two dark forms showed in front of the billboards, didn't pause to pick anything up. The steps came near, cigarette tips glowed.

A voice said softly: ' 'Lo there, sweets. Yo' want to change yo'r boy frien', honey?'

The girl shrank behind Pete Anglich. One of the negroes laughed gently, waved the red end of his cigarette.

'Hell, it's a white gal,' the other one said quickly. 'Le's dust.'

They went on, chuckling. At the corner they turned, were gone.

'There you are,' Pete Anglich growled. 'Shows you where you are.' His voice was hard, angry. 'Oh, hell, stay here and I'll get your damn pay-off for you.'

He left the girl and went lightly along close to the front of the apartment house. At the edge of the billboards he stopped, probed the darkness with his eyes, saw the package. It was wrapped in dark material, not large but large enough to see. He bent down and looked under the billboards. He didn't see anything behind them.

He went on four steps, leaned down and picked up the package, felt cloth and two thick rubber bands. He stood quite still, listening.

Distant traffic hummed on a main street. A light burned across the street in a rooming house, behind a glass-panelled door. A window was open and dark above it.

A woman's voice screamed shrilly behind him.

He stiffened, whirled, and the light hit him between the eyes. It came from the dark window across the street, a blinding white shaft that impaled him against the billboard.

His face leered in it, his eyes blinked. He didn't move any more.

Shoes dropped on cement and a smaller spot stabbed at him sideways from the end of the billboards. Behind the spot a casual voice spoke: 'Don't shift an eyelash, bud. You're all wrapped up in law.'

Men with revolvers out closed in on him from both ends of the line of billboards. Heels clicked far off on concrete. Then it was silent for a moment. Then a car with a red spotlight swung around the corner and bore down on the group of men with Pete Anglich in their midst.

The man with the casual voice said: 'I'm Angus, detective-lieutenant. I'll take the packet, if you don't mind. And if you'll just keep your hands together a minute — '

The handcuffs clicked dryly on Pete Anglich's wrists.

He listened hard for the sound of the heels far off, running away. But there was too much noise around him now.

Doors opened and dark people began to boil out of the houses.

3

John Vidaury was six feet two inches in height and had the most perfect profile in Hollywood. He was dark, winsome, romantic, with an interesting touch of grey at his temples. His shoulders were wide, his hips narrow. He had the waist of an English Guards officer, and his dinner clothes fit him so beautifully that it hurt.

So he looked at Pete Anglich as if he was about to apologize for not knowing him. Pete Anglich looked at his handcuffs, at his worn shoes on the thick rug, at the tall chiming clock against the wall. There was a flush on his face and his eyes were bright.

In a smooth, clear, modulated voice Vidaury said, 'No, I've never seen him before.' He smiled at Pete Anglich.

Angus, the plain clothes lieutenant, leaned against one end of a carved library table and snapped a finger against the brim of his hat. Two other detectives stood near a side wall. A fourth sat at a small desk with a stenographer's notebook in front of him.

Angus said: 'Oh, we just thought you might know him. We can't get much of anything out of him.'

Vidaury raised his eyebrows, smiled very faintly. 'Really! I'm surprised at that.' He went around collecting glasses, and took them over to a tray, started to mix more drinks.

'It happens,' Angus said.

'I thought you had ways,' Vidaury said delicately, pouring Scotch into the glasses.

Angus looked at a fingernail. 'When I say he won't tell us anything, Mr Vidaury, I mean anything that counts. He says his name is Pete Anglich, that he used to be a fighter, but hasn't fought for several years. Up to about a year ago he was a private detective, but has no work now. He won some money in a crap game and got drunk, and was just wandering about. That's how he happened to be on Noon Street. He saw the package tossed out of your car and picked it up. We can charge him with vagrancy, but that's about all.'

'It could happen that way,' Vidaury said softly. He carried the glasses two at a time to the four detectives, lifted his own, and nodded slightly before he drank. He drank gracefully, with a superb elegance of movement. 'No, I don't know him,' he said again. 'Frankly, he doesn't look like an acid-thrower to me.' He waved a hand. 'So I'm afraid bringing him here —'

Pete Anglich lifted his head suddenly, stared at Vidaury. His voice sneered.

'It's a great compliment, Vidaury. They don't often use up the time of four coppers taking prisoners around to call on people.'

Vidaury smiled amiably. 'That's Hollywood,' he smiled. 'After all, one has a reputation.'

'Had,' Pete Anglich said. 'Your last picture was a pain where you don't tell the ladies.'

Angus stiffened. Vidaury's face went white. He put his glass down slowly, let his hand fall to his side. He walked springily across the rug and stood in front of Pete Anglich.

'That's your opinion,' he said harshly, 'but I warn you —'

Pete Anglich scowled at him. 'Listen, big shot. You put a grand on the line because some punk promised to throw acid at you if you didn't. I picked up the grand, but I didn't get any of your nice new money. So you got it back. You get ten grand worth of publicity and it won't cost you a nickel. I call that pretty swell.'

Angus said sharply, 'That's enough from you, mug.'

'Yeah?' Pete Anglich sneered. 'I thought you wanted me to talk. Well, I'm talking, and I hate pikers, see?'

Vidaury breathed hard. Very suddenly he balled his fist and swung at Pete Anglich's jaw. Pete Anglich's head rolled under the blow, and his eyes blinked shut, then wide open. He shook himself and said coolly: 'Elbow up and thumb down, Vidaury. You break a hand hitting a guy that way.'

Vidaury stepped back and shook his head, looked at his thumb. His face lost its whiteness. His smile stole back.

'I'm sorry,' he said contritely. 'I am very sorry. I'm not used

to being insulted. As I don't know this man, perhaps you'd
better take him away, Lieutenant. Handcuffed, too. Not very
sporting, was it?'

'Tell that to your polo ponies,' Pete Anglich said. 'I don't
bruise so easy.'

Angus walked over to him, tapped his shoulder. 'Up on the
dogs, bo. Let's drift. You're not used to nice people, are you?'

'No. I like bums,' Pete Anglich said.

He stood up slowly, scuffed at the pile of the carpet.

The two dicks against the wall fell in beside him, and they
walked away down the huge room, under an arch. Angus and
the other man came behind. They waited in the small private
lobby for the elevator to come up.

'What was the idea?' Angus snapped. 'Getting gashouse with
him?'

Pete Anglich laughed. 'Jumpy,' he said. 'Just jumpy.'

The elevator came up and they rode down to the huge, silent
lobby of the Chester Towers. Two house detectives lounged at
the end of the marble desk, two clerks stood alert behind
it.

Pete Anglich lifted his manacled hands in the fighter's
salute. 'What, no newshawks yet?' he jeered. 'Vidaury won't
like hush-hush on this.'

'Keep goin', smarty,' one of the dicks snapped, jerking his
arm.

They went down a corridor and out of a side entrance to a
narrow street that dropped almost sheer to treetops. Beyond
the treetops the lights of the city were a vast golden carpet,
stitched with brilliant splashes of red and green and blue and
purple.

Two starters whirred. Pete Anglich was pushed into the
back seat of the first car. Angus and another man got in on
either side of him. The cars drifted down the hill, turned east
on Fountain, slid quietly through the evening for mile after
mile. Fountain met Sunset, and the cars dropped downtown
towards the tall white tower of the City Hall. At the plaza

the first car swung over to Los Angeles Street and went south. The other car went on.

After a while Pete Anglich dropped the corners of his mouth and looked sideways at Angus.

'Where you taking me? This isn't the way to Headquarters.'

Angus' dark, austere face turned towards him slowly. After a moment the big detective leaned back and yawned at the night. He didn't answer.

The car slid along Los Angeles to Fifth, east to San Pedro, south again for block after block, quiet blocks and loud blocks, blocks where silent men sat on shaky front porches and blocks where noisy young toughs of both colours snarled and wise-cracked at one another in front of cheap restaurants and drug-stores and beer parlours full of slot machines.

At Santa Barbara the police car turned east again, drifted slowly along the kerb to Noon Street. It stopped at the corner above the lunch wagon. Pete Anglich's face tightened again, but he didn't say anything.

'Okay,' Angus drawled. 'Take the nippers off.'

The dick on Pete Anglich's other side dug a key out of his vest, unlocked the handcuffs, jangled them pleasantly before he put them away on his hip. Angus swung the door open and stepped out of the car.

'Out,' he said over his shoulder.

Pete Anglich got out. Angus walked a little way from the street light, stopped, beckoned. His hand moved under his coat, came out with a gun. He said softly: 'Had to play it this way. Otherwise we'd tip the town. Pearson's the only one that knows you. Any ideas?'

Pete Anglich took his gun, shook his head slowly, slid the gun under his own coat, keeping his body between it and the car at the kerb behind.

'The stake-out was spotted, I guess,' he said slowly. 'There was a girl hanging around there, but maybe that just happened, too.'

Angus stared at him silently for a moment, then nodded and

went back to the car. The door slammed shut, and the car drifted off down the street and picked up speed.

Pete Anglich walked along Santa Barbara to Central, south on Central. After a while a bright sign glared at him in violet letters – JUGGERNAUT CLUB. He went up broad carpeted stairs towards noise and dance music.

4

The girl had to go sideways to get between the close-set tables around the small dance floor. Her hips touched the back of a man's shoulder and he reached out and grabbed her hand, grinning. She smiled mechanically, pulled her hand away and came on.

She looked better in the bronze metal-cloth dress with bare arms and the brown hair curling low on her neck; better than in skyscraper heels, bare legs and thighs, the irreducible minimum above the waistline, and a dull gold opera hat tipped rakishly over one ear.

Her face looked haggard, small, pretty, shallow. Her eyes had a wide stare. The dance band made a sharp racket over the clatter of dishes, the thick hum of talk, the shuffling feet on the dance floor. The girl came slowly up to Pete Anglich's table, pulled the other chair out and sat down.

She propped her chin on the backs of her hands, put her elbows on the tablecloth, stared at him.

'Hello there,' she said in a voice that shook a little.

Pete Anglich pushed a pack of cigarettes across the table, watched her shake one loose and get it between her lips. He struck a match. She had to take it out of his hand to light her cigarette.

'Drink?'

'I'll say.'

He signalled the fuzzy-haired, almond-eyed waiter, ordered a couple of sidecars. The waiter went away. Pete Anglich leaned back on his chair and looked at one of his blunt fingertips.

The girl said very softly: 'I got your note, mister.'

'Like it?' His voice was stiffly casual. He didn't look at her.

She laughed off key. 'We've got to please the customers.'

Pete Anglich looked past her shoulder at the corner of the band shell. A man stood there smoking, beside a small microphone. He was heavily built, old for an M.C., with slick grey hair and a big nose and the thickened complexion of a steady drinker. He was smiling at everything and everybody. Pete Anglich looked at him a little while, watching the direction of his glances. He said stiffly, in the same casual voice, 'But you'd be here anyway.'

The girl stiffened, then slumped. 'You don't have to insult me, mister.'

He looked at her slowly, with an empty up-from-under look. 'You're down and out, knee-deep in nothing, baby. I've been that way often enough to know the symptoms. Besides, you got me in plenty jam tonight. I owe you a couple insults.'

The fuzzy-haired waiter came back and slid a tray on the cloth, wiped the bottoms of two glasses with a dirty towel, set them out. He went away again.

The girl put her hand around a glass, lifted it quickly and took a long drink. She shivered a little as she put the glass down. Her face was white.

'Wisecrack or something,' she said rapidly. 'Don't just sit there. I'm watched.'

Pete Anglich touched his fresh drink, smiled very deliberately towards the corner of the band shell.

'Yeah, I can imagine. Tell me about that pick-up on Noon Street.'

She reached out quickly and touched his arm. Her sharp nails dug into it. 'Not here,' she breathed. 'I don't know how you found me and I don't care. You looked like the kind of Joe that would help a girl out. I was scared stiff. But don't talk about it here. I'll do anything you want, go anywhere you want. Only not here.'

Pete Anglich took his arm from under her hand, leaned back again. His eyes were cold, but his mouth was kind.

'I get it. Trimmer's wishes. Was he tailing the job?'

She nodded quickly. 'I hadn't gone three blocks before he picked me up. He thought it was a swell gag, what I did, but he won't think so when he sees you here. That makes you wise.'

Pete Anglich sipped his drink. 'He is coming this way,' he said, coolly.

The grey-haired M.C. was moving among the tables, bowing and talking, but edging towards the one where Pete Anglich sat with the girl. The girl was staring into a big gilt mirror behind Pete Anglich's head. Her face was suddenly distorted, shattered with terror. Her lips were shaking uncontrollably.

Trimmer Waltz idled casually up to the table, leaned a hand down on it. He poked his big-veined nose at Pete Anglich. There was a soft, flat grin on his face.

'Hi, Pete. Haven't seen you around since they buried McKinley. How's tricks?'

'Not bad, not good,' Pete Anglich said huskily. 'I been on a drunk.'

Trimmer Waltz broadened his smile, turned it on the girl. She looked at him quickly, looked away, picking at the tablecloth.

Waltz's voice was soft, cooing. 'Know the little lady before — or just pick her out of the line-up?'

Pete Anglich shrugged, looked bored. 'Just wanted somebody to share a drink with, Trimmer. Sent her a note. Okay?'

'Sure. Perfect.' Waltz picked one of the glasses up, sniffed at it. He shook his head sadly. 'Wish we could serve better stuff. At four bits a throw it can't be done. How about tipping a few out of a right bottle, back in my den?'

'Both of us?' Pete Anglich asked gently.

'Both of you is right. In about five minutes. I got to circulate a little first.'

He pinched the girl's cheek, went on, with a loose swing of his tailored shoulders.

The girl said slowly, thickly, hopelessly: 'So Pete's your name. You must want to die young, Pete. Mine's Token Ware. Silly name, isn't it?'

'I like it,' Pete Anglich said softly.

The girl stared at a point below the white scar on Pete Anglich's throat. Her eyes slowly filled with tears.

Trimmer Waltz drifted among the tables, speaking to a customer here and there. He edged over to the far wall, came along it to the band shell, stood there ranging the house with his eyes until he was looking directly at Pete Anglich. He jerked his head, stepped back through a pair of thick curtains.

Pete Anglich pushed his chair back and stood up. 'Let's go,' he said.

Token Ware crushed a cigarette out in a glass tray with jerky fingers, finished the drink in her glass, stood up. They went back between the tables, along the edge of the dance floor, over to the side of the band shell.

The curtains opened on to a dim hallway with doors on both sides. A shabby red carpet masked the floor. The walls were chipped, the doors cracked.

'The one at the end on the left,' Token Ware whispered.

They came to it. Pete Anglich knocked. Trimmer Waltz's voice called out to come in. Pete Anglich stood a moment looking at the door, then turned his head and looked at the girl with his eyes hard and narrow. He pushed the door open, gestured at her. They went in.

The room was not very light. A small oblong reading lamp on the desk shed glow on polished wood, but less on the shabby red carpet, and the long heavy red drapes across the outer wall. The air was close, with a thick, sweetish smell of liquor.

Trimmer Waltz sat behind the desk, with his hands touched a tray that contained a cut-glass decanter, some gold-veined glasses, an ice bucket and a siphon of charged water.

He smiled, rubbed one side of his big nose.

'Park yourselves, folks. Liqueur Scotch at six-ninety a fifth. That's what it costs me – wholesale.'

Pete Anglich shut the door, looked slowly around the room, at the floor-length window drapes, at the unlighted ceiling light. He unbuttoned the top button of his coat with a slow, easy movement.

'Hot in here,' he said softly. 'Any windows behind those drapes?'

The girl sat in a round chair on the opposite side of the desk from Waltz. He smiled at her very gently.

'Good idea,' Waltz said. 'Open one up, will you?'

Pete Anglich went past the end of the desk, towards the curtains. As he got beyond Waltz, his hand went up under his coat and touched the butt of his gun. He moved softly towards the red drapes. The tips of wide, square-toed black shoes just barely showed under the curtains, in the shadow between the curtains and the wall.

Pete Anglich reached the curtains, put his left hand out and jerked them open.

The shoes on the floor against the wall were empty. Waltz laughed dryly behind Pete Anglich. Then a thick, cold voice said: 'Put 'em high, boy.'

The girl made a strangled sound, not quite a scream. Pete Anglich dropped his hands and turned slowly and looked. The negro was enormous in stature, gorilla-like, and wore a baggy checked suit that made him even more enormous. He had come soundlessly on shoeless feet out of a closet door, and his right hand almost covered a huge black gun.

Trimmer Waltz held a gun too, a Savage. The two men stared quietly at Pete Anglich. Pete Anglich put his hands up in the air, his eyes blank, his small mouth set hard.

The negro in the checked suit came towards him in long, loose strides, pressed the gun against his chest, then reached under his coat. His hand came out with Pete Anglich's gun. He dropped it behind him on the floor. He shifted his own gun casually and hit Pete Anglich on the side of the jaw with the flat of it.

Pete Anglich staggered and the salt taste of blood came under his tongue. He blinked, said thickly: 'I'll remember you a long time, big boy.'

The negro grinned. 'Not so long, pal. Not so long.'

He hit Pete Anglich again with the gun, then suddenly he jammed it into a side pocket and his two big hands shot out, clamped themselves on Pete Anglich's throat.

'When they're tough I likes to squeeze 'em,' he said almost softly.

Thumbs that felt as big and hard as doorknobs pressed into the arteries on Pete Anglich's neck. The face before him and above him grew enormous, an enormous shadowy face with a wide grin in the middle of it. It waved in lessening light, an unreal, a fantastic face.

Pete Anglich hit the face, with puny blows, the blows of a toy balloon. His fists didn't feel anything as they hit the face. The big man twisted him around and put a knee into his back, and bent him down over the knee.

There was no sound for a while except the thunder of blood threshing in Pete Anglich's head. Then, far away, he seemed to hear a girl scream thinly. From still farther away the voice of Trimmer Waltz muttered: 'Easy now, Rufe. Easy.'

A vast blackness shot with hot red filled Pete Anglich's world. The darkness grew silent. Nothing moved in it now, not even blood.

The negro lowered Pete Anglich's limp body to the floor, stepped back and rubbed his hands together.

'Yeah, I likes to squeeze 'em,' he said.

5

The negro in the check suit sat on the side of the daybed and picked languidly at a five-stringed banjo. His large face was solemn and peaceful, a little sad. He plucked the banjo strings slowly, with his bare fingers, his head on one side, a crumpled cigarette-end sticking barely past his lips at one corner of his mouth.

Low down in his throat he was making a kind of droning sound. He was singing.

A cheap electric clock on the mantel said 11.35. It was a small living-room with bright, overstuffed furniture, a red floor lamp with a cluster of French dolls at its base, a gay carpet with large diamond shapes in it, two curtained windows with a mirror between them.

A door at the back was ajar. A door near it opening into the hall was shut.

Pete Anglich lay on his back on the floor, with his mouth open and his arms outflung. His breath was a thick snore. His eyes were shut, and his face in the reddish glow of the lamp looked flushed and feverish.

The negro put the banjo down out of his immense hands, stood up and yawned and stretched. He walked across the room and looked at a calendar over the mantel.

'This ain't August,' he said disgustedly.

He tore a leaf from the calendar, rolled it into a ball and threw it at Pete Anglich's face. It hit the unconscious man's cheek. He didn't stir. The negro spat the cigarette-end into his palm, held his palm out flat, and flicked a fingernail at it, sent it sailing in the same direction as the paper ball.

He loafed a few steps and leaned down, fingering a bruise on Pete Anglich's temple. He pressed the bruise, grinning softly. Pete Anglich didn't move.

The negro straightened and kicked the unconscious man in the ribs, thoughtfully, over and over again, not very hard. Pete Anglich moved a little, gurgled, and rolled his head to one side. The negro looked pleased, left him, went back to the daybed. He carried his banjo over to the hall door and leaned it against the wall. There was a gun lying on a newspaper on a small table. He went through a partly open inner door and came back with a pint bottle of gin, half full. He rubbed the bottle over carefully with a handkerchief, set it on the mantel.

'About time now, pal,' he mused out loud. 'When you wake

up, maybe you don't feel so good. Maybe need a shot. . . . Hey, I gotta better hunch.'

He reached for the bottle again, went down on one big knee, poured gin over Pete Anglich's mouth and chin, slopped it loosely on the front of his shirt. He stood the bottle on the floor, after wiping it off again, and flicked the glass stopper under the daybed.

'Grab it, white boy,' he said softly. 'Prints don't never hurt.'

He got the newspaper with the gun on it, slid the gun off on the carpet, and moved it with his foot until it lay just out of reach of Pete Anglich's outflung hand.

He studied the layout carefully from the door, nodded, picked his banjo up. He opened the door, peeped out, then looked back.

'So long, pal,' he said softly. 'Time for me to breeze. You ain't got a lot of future comin' but what you got you get sudden.'

He shut the door, went along the hallway to stairs and down the stairs. Radios made faint sound behind shut doors. The entrance lobby of the apartment house was empty. The negro in the check suit slipped into a pay booth in the dark corner of the lobby, dropped his nickel and dialled.

A heavy voice said: 'Police department.'

The negro put his lips close to the transmitter and got a whine into his voice.

'This the cops? Say, there's been a shootin' scrape in the Calliope Apartments, 246 East 48th, Apartment 4-B. Got it . . . ?'

He hung up quickly, giggling, ran down the front steps of the apartment house and jumped into a small, dirty sedan. He kicked it to life and drove towards Central Avenue. He was a block from Central Avenue when the red eye of a prowl car swung around from Central Avenue on to East 48th Street.

The negro in the sedan chuckled and went on his way. He was singing down in his throat when the prowl car whirred past him.

The instant the door latch clicked Pete Anglich opened his eyes half-way. He turned his head slowly, and a grin of pain came on his face and stayed on it, but he kept on turning his head until he could see the emptiness of one end of the room and the middle. He tipped his head far back on the floor, saw the rest of the room.

He rolled towards the gun and took hold of it. It was his own gun. He sat up and snapped the gate open mechanically. His face stiffened out of the grin. One shell in the gun had been fired. The barrel smelled of powder fumes.

He came to his feet and crept towards the slightly open inner door, keeping his head low. When he reached the door he bent still lower, and slowly pushed the door wide open. Nothing happened. He looked into a bedroom with twin beds, made up and covered with rose damask with a gold design in it.

Somebody lay on one of the beds. A woman. She didn't move. The hard, tight grin came back on Pete Anglich's face. He rose straight up and walked softly on the balls of his feet over to the side of the bed. A door beyond was open on a bathroom, but no sound came from it. Pete Anglich looked down at the coloured girl on the bed.

He caught his breath and let it out slowly. The girl was dead. Her eyes were half open, uninterested, her hands lazy at her sides. Her legs were twisted a little and bare skin showed above one sheer stocking, below the short skirt. A green hat lay on the floor. She had four-and-a-half-inch French heels. There was a scent of Midnight Narcissus in the room. He remembered the girl outside the Surprise Hotel.

She was quite dead, dead long enough for the blood to have clotted over the powder-scorched hole below her left breast.

Pete Anglich went back to the living-room, grabbed up the gin bottle, and emptied it without stopping or choking. He stood a moment, breathing hard, thinking. The gun hung slack in his left hand. His small, tight mouth hardly showed at all.

He worked his fingers around on the glass of the gin bottle, tossed it empty on top of the daybed, slid his gun into the underarm holster, went to the door and stepped quietly into the hall.

The hall was long and dim and yawning with the chill air. A single bracket light loomed yellowly at the top of the stairs. A screen door led to a balcony over the front porch of the building. There was a grey splash of cold moonlight on one corner of the screen.

Pete Anglich went softly down the stairs to the front hall, put his hand out to the knob of the glass door.

A red spot hit the front of the door. It sifted a hard red glare through the glass and the sleazy curtain that masked it.

Pete Anglich slid down the door, below the panel, hunched along the wall to the side. His eyes ranged the place swiftly, held on the dark telephone booth.

'Man trap,' he said softly, and dodged over to the booth, into it. He crouched and almost shut the door.

Steps slammed on the porch and the front door squeaked open. The steps hammered into the hallway, stopped.

A heavy voice said: 'All quiet, huh? May be a phoney.'

Another voice said: 'Four-B. Let's give it the dust, anyway.'

The steps went along the lower hall, came back. They sounded on the stairs going up. They drummed in the upper hall.

Pete Anglich pushed the door of the booth back, slid over to the front door, crouched and squinted against the red glare.

The prowl car at the kerb was a dark bulk. Its headlights burned along the cracked sidewalk. He couldn't see into it. He sighed, opened the door and walked quickly, but not too quickly, down the wooden steps from the porch.

The prowl car was empty, with both front doors hanging open. Shadowy forms were converging cautiously from across the street. Pete Anglich marched straight to the prowl car and got into it. He shut the doors quietly, stepped on the starter, threw the car in gear.

He drove off past the gathering crowd of neighbours. At the first corner he turned and switched off the red spot. Then he drove fast, wound in and out of blocks, away from Central, after a while turned back towards it.

When he was near its lights and chatter and traffic he pulled over to the side of the dusty tree-lined street, left the prowl car standing.

He walked towards Central.

6

Trimmer Waltz cradled the phone with his left hand. He put his right index finger along the edge of his upper lip, pushed the lip out of the way, and rubbed his finger slowly along his teeth and gums. His shallow, colourless eyes looked across the desk at the big negro in the check suit.

'Lovely,' he said in a dead voice. 'Lovely. He got away before the law jumped him. A very swell job, Rufe.'

The negro took a cigar stub out of his mouth and crushed it between a huge flat thumb and a huge flat forefinger.

'Hell, he was out cold,' he snarled. 'The prowlies passed me before I got to Central. Hell, he *can't* get away.'

'That was him talking,' Waltz said lifelessly. He opened the top drawer of his desk and laid his heavy Savage in front of him.

The negro looked at the Savage. His eyes got dull and lightless, like obsidian. His lips puckered and gouged at each other.

'That gal's been cuttin' corners on me with three, four other guys,' he grumbled. 'I owed her the slug. Oky-doke. That's jake. Now, I go out and collect me the smart monkey.'

He started to get up. Waltz barely touched the butt of his gun with two fingers. He shook his head, and the negro sat down again. Waltz spoke.

'He got away, Rufe. And you called the buttons to find a dead woman. Unless they get him with the gun on him – one chance in a thousand – there's no way to tie it to him. That makes you the fall guy. You live there.'

The negro grinned and kept his dull eyes on the Savage.

He said: 'That makes me get cold feet. And my feet are big enough to get plenty cold. Guess I take me a powder, huh?'

Waltz sighed. He said thoughtfully: 'Yeah, I guess you leave town for a while. From Glendale. The 'Frisco late train will be about right.'

The negro looked sulky. 'Nix on 'Frisco, boss. I put my thumbs on a frail there. She croaked. Nix on 'Frisco, boss.'

'You've got ideas, Rufe,' Waltz said calmly. He rubbed the side of his veined nose with one finger, then slicked his grey hair back with his palm. 'I see them in your big brown eyes. Forget it. I'll take care of you. Get the car in the alley. We'll figure the angles on the way to Glendale.'

The negro blinked and wiped cigar ash off his chin with his huge hand.

'And better leave your big shiny gun here,' Waltz added. 'It needs a rest.'

Rufe reached back and slowly drew his gun from a hip pocket. He pushed it across the polished wood of the desk with one finger. There was a faint, sleepy smile at the back of his eyes.

'Okay, boss,' he said, almost dreamily.

He went across to the door, opened it, and went out. Waltz stood up and stepped over to the closet, put on a dark felt hat and a lightweight overcoat, a pair of dark gloves. He dropped the Savage into his left-hand pocket, Rufe's gun into the right. He went out of the room down the hall towards the sound of the dance band.

At the end he parted the curtains just enough to peer through. The orchestra was playing a waltz. There was a good crowd, a quiet crowd for Central Avenue. Waltz sighed, watched the dancers for a moment, let the curtains fall together again.

He went back along the hall past his office to a door at the end that gave on stairs. Another door at the bottom of the stairs opened on a dark alley behind the building.

Waltz closed the door gently, stood in the darkness against the wall. The sound of an idling motor came to him, the light clatter of loose tappets. The alley was blind at one end, at the other turned at right angles towards the front of the building. Some of the light from Central Avenue splashed on a brick wall at the end of the cross alley, beyond the waiting car, a small sedan that looked battered and dirty even in the darkness.

Waltz reached his right hand into his overcoat pocket, took out Rufe's gun and held it down in the cloth of his overcoat. He walked to the sedan soundlessly, went around to the right-hand door, opened it to get in.

Two huge hands came out of the car and took hold of his throat. Hard hands, hands with enormous strength in them. Waltz made a faint gurgling sound before his head was bent back and his almost blind eyes were groping at the sky.

Then his right hand moved, moved like a hand that had nothing to do with his stiff, straining body, his tortured neck, his bulging blind eyes. It moved forward cautiously, delicately, until the muzzle of the gun it held pressed against something soft. It explored the something soft carefully without haste, seemed to be making sure just what it was.

Trimmer Waltz didn't see, he hardly felt. He didn't breathe. But his hand obeyed his brain like a detached force beyond the reach of Rufe's terrible hands. Waltz's finger squeezed the trigger.

The hands fell slack on his throat, dropped away. He staggered back, almost fell across the alley, hit the far wall with his shoulder. He straightened slowly, gasping deep down in his tortured lungs. He began to shake.

He hardly noticed the big gorilla's body fall out of the car and slam the concrete at his feet. It lay at his feet, limp, enormous, but no longer menacing. No longer important.

Waltz dropped the gun on the sprawled body. He rubbed his throat gently for a little while. His breathing was deep, racking, noisy. He searched the inside of his mouth with his tongue, tasted blood. His eyes looked up wearily at the indigo slit of the night sky above the alley.

After a while he said huskily: 'I thought of that, Rufe. . . . You see, I thought of that.'

He laughed, shuddered, adjusted his coat collar, went around the sprawled body to the car and reached in to switch the motor off. He started back along the alley to the rear door of the Juggernaut Club.

A man stepped out of the shadows at the back of the car. Waltz's left hand flashed to his overcoat pocket. Shiny metal blinked at him. He let his hand fall loosely at his side.

Pete Anglich said: 'Thought that call would bring you out, Trimmer. Thought you might come this way. Nice going.'

After a moment Waltz said thickly: 'He choked me. It was self-defence.'

'Sure. There's two of us with sore necks. Mine's a pip.'

'What do you want, Pete?'

'You tried to frame me for bumping off a girl.'

Waltz laughed suddenly, almost crazily. He said quietly: 'When I'm crowded I get nasty, Pete. You should know that. Better lay off little Token Ware.'

Pete Anglich moved his gun so that the light flickered on the barrel. He came up to Waltz, pushed the gun against his stomach.

'Rufe's dead,' he said softly. 'Very convenient. Where's the girl?'

'What's it to you?'

'Don't be a bunny. I'm wise. You tried to pick some jack off John Vidaury. I stepped in front of Token. I want to know the rest of it.'

Waltz stood very still with the gun pressing his stomach. His fingers twisted in the gloves.

'Okay,' he said dully. 'How much to button your lip – and keep it buttoned?'

'Couple of centuries. Rufe lifted my poke.'

'What does it buy me?' Waltz asked slowly.

'Not a damn thing. I want the girl, too.'

Waltz said very gently: 'Five C's. But not the girl. Five C's is heavy dough for a Central Avenue punk. Be smart and take it, and forget the rest.'

The gun went away from his stomach. Pete Anglich circled

him deftly, patted pockets, took the Savage, made a gesture with his left hand, holding it.

'Sold,' he said grudgingly. 'What's a girl between pals? Feed it to me.'

'Have to go up to the office,' Waltz said.

Pete Anglich laughed shortly. 'Better play ball, Trimmer. Lead on.'

They went back along the upstairs hall. The dance band beyond the distant curtains was wailing a Duke Ellington lament, a forlorn monotone of stifled brasses, bitter violins, softly clicking gourds. Waltz opened his office door, snapped the light on, went across to his desk and sat down. He tilted his hat back, smiled, opened a drawer with a key.

Pete Anglich watched him, reached back to turn the key in the door, went along the wall to the closet and looked into it, went behind Waltz to the curtains that masked the windows. He still had his gun out.

He came back to the end of the desk. Waltz was pushing a loose sheaf of bills away from him.

Pete Anglich ignored the money, leaned down over the end of the desk.

'Keep that and give me the girl, Trimmer.'

Waltz shook his head, kept on smiling.

'The Vidaury squeeze was a grand, Trimmer – or started with a grand. Noon Street is almost in your alley. Do you have to scare women into doing your dirty work? I think you wanted something on the girl, so you could make her say uncle.'

Waltz narrowed his eyes a little, pointed to the sheaf of bills.

Pete Anglich said slowly: 'A shabby, lonesome, scared kid. Probably lives in a cheap furnished room. No friends, or she wouldn't be working in your joint. Nobody would wonder about her, except me. You wouldn't have put her in a house, would you, Trimmer?'

'Take your money and beat it,' Waltz said thinly. 'You know what happens to rats in this district.'

'Sure, they run night clubs,' Pete Anglich said gently.

He put his gun down, started to reach for the money. His fist doubled, swept upward casually. His elbow went up with the punch, the fist turned, landed almost delicately on the angle of Waltz's jaw.

Waltz became a loose bag of clothes. His mouth fell open. His hat fell off the back of his head. Pete Anglich stared at him, grumbled: 'Lot of good that does me.'

The room was very still. The dance band sounded faintly, like a turned-down radio. Pete Anglich moved behind Waltz and reached down under his coat into his breast pocket. He took a wallet out, shook out money, a driver's licence, a police pistol permit, several insurance cards.

He put the stuff back, stared morosely at the desk, rubbed a thumbnail on his jaw. There was a shiny buff memo pad in front of him. Impressions of writing showed on the top blank sheet. He held it sideways against the light, then picked up a pencil and began to make light loose strokes across the paper. Writing came out dimly. When the sheet was shaded all over Pete Anglich read: 4623 Noon Street. Ask for Reno.

He tore the sheet off, folded it into a pocket, picked his gun up and crossed to the door. He reversed the key, locked the room from the outside, went back to the stairs and down them to the alley.

The body of the negro lay as it had fallen, between the small sedan and the dark wall. The alley was empty. Pete Anglich stooped, searched the dead man's pockets, came up with a roll of money. He counted the money in the dim light of a match, separated eighty-seven dollars from what there was, and started to put the few remaining bills back. A piece of torn paper fluttered to the pavement. One side only was torn, jaggedly.

Pete Anglich crouched beside the car, struck another match, looked at a half-sheet from a buff memo pad on which was written, beginning with the tear: ' — t. Ask for Reno.'

He clicked his teeth and let the match fall. 'Better,' he said softly.

He got into the car, started it and drove out of the alley.

7

The number was on a front-door transom, faintly lit from behind, the only light the house showed. It was a big frame house, in the block above where the stake-out had been. The windows in front were closely curtained. Noise came from behind them, voices and laughter, the high-pitched whine of a coloured girl's singing. Cars were parked along the kerb, on both sides of the street.

A tall thin negro in dark clothes and gold pince-nez opened the door. There was another door behind him, shut. He stood in a dark box between the two doors.

Pete Anglich said: 'Reno?'

The tall negro nodded, said nothing.

'I've come for the girl Rufe left, the white girl.'

The tall negro stood a moment quite motionless, looking over Pete Anglich's head. When he spoke, his voice was a lazy rustle of sound that seemed to come from somewhere else.

'Come in and shut the do'.'

Pete Anglich stepped into the house, shut the outer door behind him. The tall negro opened the inner door. It was thick, heavy. When he opened it sound and light jumped at them. A purplish light. He went through the inner door, into a hallway.

The purplish light came through a broad arch from a long living-room. It had heavy velour drapes, davenports and deep chairs, a glass bar in the corner, and a white-coated negro behind the bar. Four couples lounged about the room drinking; slim, slick-haired negro sheiks and girls with bare arms, sheer silk legs, plucked eyebrows. The soft, purplish light made the scene unreal.

Reno stared vaguely past Pete Anglich's shoulder, dropped

his heavy-lidded eyes, said wearily: 'You says which?'

The negroes beyond the arch were quiet, staring. The barman stooped and put his hands down under the bar.

Pete Anglich put his hand into his pocket slowly, brought out a crumpled piece of paper.

'This any help?'

Reno took the paper, studied it. He reached languidly into his vest and brought out another piece of the same colour. He fitted the pieces together. His head went back and he looked at the ceiling.

'Who send you?'

'Trimmer.'

'I don't like it,' the tall negro said. 'He done write my name. I don' like that. That ain't sma't. Apa't from that I guess I check you.'

He turned and started up a long, straight flight of stairs. Pete Anglich followed him. One of the negro youths in the living-room snickered loudly.

Reno stopped suddenly, turned and went back down the steps, through the arch. He went up to the snickerer.

'This is business,' he said exhaustedly. 'Ain't no white folks comin' heah. Git me?'

The boy who had laughed said: 'Okay, Reno,' and lifted a tall, misted glass.

Reno came up the stairs again, talking to himself. Along the upper hall were many closed doors. There was faint pink light from flame-coloured wall lamps. At the end Reno took a key out and unlocked the door.

He stood aside. 'Git her out,' he said tersely. 'I don' handle no white cargo heah.'

Pete Anglich stepped past him into a bedroom. An orange floor lamp glowed in the far corner, near a flounced, gaudy bed. The windows were shut, the air heavy, sickish.

Token Ware lay on her side on the bed, with her face to the wall, sobbing quietly.

Pete Anglich stepped to the side of the bed, touched her. She whirled, cringed. Her head jerked around at him, her eyes dilated, her mouth half open as if to yell.

'Hello, there,' he said quietly, very gently. 'I've been looking all over for you.'

The girl stared back at him. Slowly all the fear went out of her face.

8

The *News* photographer held the flashbulb holder high up in his left hand, leaned down over his camera. 'Now, the smile, Mr Vidaury,' he said. 'The sad one – that one that makes 'em pant.'

Vidaury turned in the chair and set his profile. He smiled at the girl in the red hat, then turned his face to the camera with the smile still on.

The bulb flared and the shutter clicked.

'Not bad, Mr Vidaury. I've seen you do better.'

'I've been under a great strain,' Vidaury said gently.

'I'll say. Acid in the face is no fun,' the photographer said.

The girl in the red hat tittered, then coughed, behind a gauntleted glove with red stitching on the back.

The photographer packed his stuff together. He was an oldish man in shiny blue serge, with sad eyes. He shook his grey head and straightened his hat.

'No, acid in the puss is no fun,' he said. 'Well, I hope our boys can see you in the morning, Mr Vidaury.'

'Delighted,' Vidaury said wearily. 'Just tell them to ring me from the lobby before they come up. And have a drink on your way out.'

'I'm crazy,' the photographer said. 'I don't drink.'

He hoisted his camera bag over his shoulder and trudged down the room. A small Jap in a white coat appeared from nowhere and let him out, then went away.

'Acid in the puss,' the girl in the red hat said. 'Ha, ha, ha! That's positively excruciating, if a nice girl may say so. Can I have a drink?'

'Nobody's stopping you,' Vidaury growled.

'Nobody ever did, sweets.'

She walked sinuously over to a table with a square Chinese tray on it. She mixed a stiff one. Vidaury said half absently: 'That should be all till morning. The *Bulletin*, the *Press-Tribune*, the three wire services, the *News*. Not bad.'

'I'd call it a perfect score,' the girl in the red hat said.

Vidaury scowled at her. 'But nobody caught,' he said softly, 'except an innocent passer-by. *You* wouldn't know anything about this squeeze, would you, Irma?'

Her smile was lazy, but cold. 'Me take you for a measly grand? Be your forty years plus, Johnny. I'm a home-run hitter, always.'

Vidaury stood up and crossed the room to a carved wood cabinet, unlocked a small drawer and took a large ball of crystal out of it. He went back to his chair, sat down, and leaned forward, holding the ball in his palms and staring into it, almost vacantly.

The girl in the red hat watched him over the rim of her glass. Her eyes widened, got a little glassy.

'Hell! He's gone psychic on the folks,' she breathed. She put her glass down with a sharp slap on the tray, drifted over to his side and leaned down. Her voice was cooing, edged. 'Ever hear of senile decay, Johnny? It happens to exceptionally wicked men in their forties. They get gaga over flowers and toys, cut out paper dolls and play with glass balls. . . . Can it, for God's sake, Johnny! You're not a punk yet.'

Vidaury stared fixedly into the crystal ball. He breathed slowly, deeply.

The girl in the red hat leaned still closer to him. 'Let's go riding, Johnny,' she cooed. 'I like the night air. It makes me remember my tonsils.'

'I don't want to go riding,' Vidaury said vaguely. 'I – I feel something. Something imminent.'

The girl bent suddenly and knocked the ball out of his hands. It thudded heavily on the floor, rolled sluggishly in the deep nap of the rug.

Vidaury shot to his feet, his face convulsed.

'I want to go riding, handsome,' the girl said coolly. 'It's a nice night, and you've got a nice car. So I want to go riding.'

Vidaury stared at her with hate in his eyes. Slowly he smiled. The hate went away. He reached out and touched her lips with two fingers.

'Of course we'll go riding, baby,' he said softly.

He got the ball, locked it up in the cabinet, went through an inner door. The girl in the red hat opened a bag and touched her lips with rouge, pursed them, made a face at herself in the mirror of her compact, found a rough wool coat in beige, braided with red, and shrugged into it carefully, tossed a scarf-like collar end over her shoulder.

Vidaury came back with a hat and coat on, a fringed muffler hanging down his coat.

They went down the room.

'Let's sneak out the back way,' he said at the door. 'In case any more newshawks are hanging around.'

'Why, Johnny!' the girl in the red hat raised mocking eyebrows. 'People saw me come in, saw me here. Surely you wouldn't want them to think your girl friend stayed the night?'

'Hell!' Vidaury said violently and wrenched the door open.

The telephone bell jangled back in the room. Vidaury swore again, took his hand from the door and stood waiting while the little Jap in the white jacket came in and answered the phone.

The boy put the phone down, smiled deprecatingly and gestured with his hands.

'You take, prease? I not understand.'

Vidaury walked back and lifted the instrument. He said: 'Yes? This is John Vidaury.' He listened.

Slowly his fingers tightened on the phone. His whole face tightened, got white. He said slowly, thickly: 'Hold the line a minute.'

He put the phone down on its side, put his hand down on the

table and leaned on it. The girl in the red hat came up behind him.

'Bad news, handsome? You look like a washed egg.'

Vidaury turned his head slowly and stared at her. 'Get the hell out of here,' he said tonelessly.

She laughed. He straightened, took a single long step and slapped her across the mouth, hard.

'I said, get the hell out of here,' he repeated in an utterly dead voice.

She stopped laughing and touched her lips with fingers in the gauntleted glove. Her eyes were round, but not shocked.

'Why, Johnny. You sweep me right off my feet,' she said wonderingly. 'You're simply terrific. Of course I'll go.'

She turned quickly, with a light toss of her head, went back along the room to the door, waved her hand, and went out.

Vidaury was not looking at her when she waved. He lifted the phone as soon as the door clicked shut after her, said into it grimly: 'Get over here, Waltz – and get over here quick!'

He dropped the phone on its cradle, stood a moment blank-eyed. He went back through the inner door, reappeared in a moment without his hat and overcoat. He held a thick, short automatic in his hand. He slipped it nose-down into the inside breast pocket of his dinner jacket, lifted the phone again slowly, said into it coldly and firmly: 'If a Mr Anglich calls to see me, send him up. Anglich.' He spelled the name out, put the phone down carefully, and sat down in the easy chair beside it.

He folded his arms and waited.

9

The white-jacketed Japanese boy opened the door, bobbed his head, smiled, hissed politely: 'Ah, you come inside, prease. Quite so, prease.'

Pete Anglich patted Token Ware's shoulder, pushed her through the door into the long, vivid room. She looked shabby and forlorn against the background of handsome furnishings. Her eyes were reddened from crying, her mouth was smeared.

The door shut behind them and the little Japanese stole away.

They went down the stretch of thick, noiseless carpet, past quiet brooding lamps, bookcases sunk into the wall, shelves of alabaster and ivory, and porcelain and jade knick-knacks, a huge mirror framed in blue glass, and surrounded by a frieze of lovingly autographed photos, low tables with lounging chairs, high tables with flowers, more books, more chairs, more rugs – and Vidaury sitting remotely with a glass in his hand, staring at them coldly.

He moved his hand carelessly, looked the girl up and down.

'Ah, yes, the man the police had here. Of course. Something I can do for you? I heard they made a mistake.'

Pete Anglich turned a chair a little, pushed Token Ware into it. She sat down slowly, stiffly, licked her lips and stared at Vidaury with a frozen fascination.

A touch of polite distaste curled Vidaury's lips. His eyes were watchful.

Pete Anglich sat down. He drew a stick of gum out of his pocket, unwrapped it, slid it between his teeth. He looked worn, battered, tired. There were dark bruises on the side of his face and on his neck. He still needed a shave.

He said slowly: 'This is Miss Ware. The girl that was supposed to get your dough.'

Vidaury stiffened. A hand holding a cigarette began to tap restlessly on the arm of his chair. He stared at the girl, but didn't say anything. She half smiled at him, then flushed.

Pete Anglich said: 'I hang around Noon Street. I know the sharpshooters, know what kind of folks belong there and what kind don't. I saw this little girl in a lunch-wagon on Noon Street this evening. She looked uneasy and she was watching the clock. She didn't belong. When she left I followed her.'

Vidaury nodded slightly. A grey tip of ash fell off the end of his cigarette. He looked down at it vaguely, nodded again.

'She went up Noon Street,' Pete Anglich said. 'A bad street for a white girl. I found her hiding in a doorway. Then a big Duesenberg slid around the corner and doused lights, and your money was thrown out on the sidewalk. She was scared. She asked me to get it. I got it.'

Vidaury said smoothly, not looking at the girl: 'She doesn't look like a crook. Have you told the police about her? I suppose not, or you wouldn't be here.'

Pete Anglich shook his head, ground the gum around in his jaws. 'Tell the law? A couple of times nix. This is velvet for us. We want our cut.'

Vidaury started violently, then he was very still. His hand stopped beating the chair arm. His face got cold and white and grim. Then he reached up inside his dinner jacket and quietly took the short automatic out, held it on his knees. He leaned forward a little and smiled.

'Blackmailers,' he said gravely, 'are always rather interesting. How much would your cut be – and what have you got to sell?'

Pete Anglich looked thoughtfully at the gun. His jaws moved easily, crunching the gum. His eyes were unworried.

'Silence,' he said gravely. 'Just silence.'

Vidaury made a sharp sudden gesture with the gun. 'Talk,' he said. 'And talk fast. I don't like silence.'

Pete Anglich nodded, said: 'The acid-throwing threats were just a dream. You didn't get any. The extortion attempt was a phoney. A publicity stunt. That's all.' He leaned back in his chair.

Vidaury looked down the room past Pete Anglich's shoulder. He started to smile, then his face got wooden.

Trimmer Waltz had slid into the room through an open side door. He had his big Savage in his hand. He came slowly along the carpet without sound. Pete Anglich and the girl didn't see him.

Pete Anglich said: 'Phoney all the way through. Just a build-up. Guessing? Sure I am, but look a minute, see how soft it was played first – and how tough it was played afterwards after I showed in it. The girl works for Trimmer Waltz at the Juggernaut. She's down and out and she scares easily. So Waltz sends her on a caper like that. Why? Because she's supposed to be nabbed. The stake-out's all arranged. If she squawks about Waltz he laughs it off, points to the fact that the plant was almost in his alley, that it was a small stake at best, and his joint's doing all right. He points to the fact that a dumb girl goes to get it, and would he, a smart guy, pull anything like that? Certainly not.

'The cops will half believe him, and you'll make a big gesture and refuse to prosecute the girl. If she doesn't spill, you'll refuse to prosecute anyway, and you'll get your publicity just the same, either way. You need it bad, because you're slipping, and you'll get it, and all it will cost you is what you pay Waltz – or that's what you think. Is that crazy? Is that too far for a Hollywood heel to stretch? Then tell me why no Feds were on the case. Because those lads would keep on digging until they found the mouse, and then you'd be up for obstructing justice. That's why. The local law don't give a damn. They're so used to movie build-ups they just yawn and turn over and go to sleep again.'

Waltz was half-way down the room now. Vidaury didn't look at him. He looked at the girl, smiled at her faintly.

'Now, see how tough it was played after I got into it,' Pete Anglich said. 'I went to the Juggernaut and talked to the girl. Waltz got us into his office and a big ape that works for him damn near strangled me. When I came to I was in an apartment and a dead girl was there, and she was shot, and a bullet was gone from my gun. The gun was on the floor beside me, and I stank of gin, and a prowl car was booming around the corner. And Miss Ware here was locked up in a whore house on Noon Street.

'Why all that hard stuff? Because Waltz had a perfectly swell blackmail racket lined up for you, and he'd have bled you whiter than an angel's wing. As long as you had a dollar, half of it would have been his. And you'd have paid it and liked it, Vidaury. You'd have had publicity, and you'd have had protection, but how you'd have paid for it!'

Waltz was close now, almost too close. Vidaury stood up suddenly. The short gun jerked at Pete Anglich's chest. Vidaury's voice was thin, an old man's voice. He said dreamily: 'Take him, Waltz. I'm too jittery for this sort of thing.'

Pete Anglich didn't even turn. His face became the face of a wooden Indian.

Waltz put his gun into Pete Anglich's back. He stood there half smiling, with the gun against Pete Anglich's back, looking across his shoulder at Vidaury.

'Dumb, Pete,' he said dryly. 'You had enough evening already. You ought to have stayed away from here – but I figured you couldn't pass it up.'

Vidaury moved a little to one side, spread his legs, flattened his feet to the floor. There was a queer, greenish tint to his handsome face, a sick glitter in his deep eyes.

Token Ware stared at Waltz. Her eyes glittered with panic, the lids straining away from the eyeballs, showing the whites all around the iris.

Waltz said: 'I can't do anything here, Vidaury. I'd rather not walk him out alone, either. Get your hat and coat.'

Vidaury nodded very slightly. His head just barely moved. His eyes were still sick.

'What about the girl?' he asked whisperingly.

Waltz grinned, shook his head, pressed the gun hard into Pete Anglich's back.

Vidaury moved a little more to the side, spread his feet again. The thick gun was very steady in his hand, but not pointed at anything in particular.

He closed his eyes, held them shut a brief instant, then opened them wide. He said slowly, carefully: 'It looked all right as it was planned. Things just as far-fetched, just as unscrupulous, have been done before in Hollywood, often. I just didn't expect it to lead to hurting people, to killing. I'm – I'm just not enough of a heel to go on with it, Waltz. Not any further. You'd better put your gun up and leave.'

Waltz shook his head; smiled a peculiar strained smile. He

stepped back from Pete Anglich and held the Savage a little to one side.

'The cards are dealt,' he said coldly. 'You'll play 'em. Get going.'

Vidaury sighed, sagged a little. Suddenly he was a lonely, forlorn man, no longer young.

'No,' he said softly. 'I'm through. The last flicker of a not-so-good reputation. It's my show, after all. Always the ham, but still my show. Put the gun up, Waltz. Take the air.'

Waltz's face got cold and hard and expressionless. His eyes became the expressionless eyes of the killer. He moved the Savage a little more.

'Get – your – hat, Vidaury,' he said very clearly.

'Sorry,' Vidaury said, and fired.

Waltz's gun flamed at the same instant, the two explosions blended. Vidaury staggered to his left and half turned, then straightened his body again.

He looked steadily at Waltz. 'Beginner's luck,' he said, and waited.

Pete Anglich had his Colt out now, but he didn't need it. Waltz fell slowly on his side. His cheek and the side of his big-veined nose pressed the nap of the rug. He moved his left arm a little, tried to throw it over his back. He gurgled, then was still.

Pete Anglich kicked the Savage away from Waltz's sprawled body.

Vidaury asked draggingly: 'Is he dead?'

Pete Anglich grunted, didn't answer. He looked at the girl. She was standing up with her back against the telephone table, the back of her hand to her mouth in the conventional attitude of startled horror. So conventional it looked silly.

Pete Anglich looked at Vidaury. He said sourly: 'Beginner's luck – yeah. But suppose you'd missed him? He was bluffing. Just wanted you in a little deeper, so you wouldn't squawk. As a matter of fact, I'm his alibi on a kill.'

Vidaury said: 'Sorry . . . I'm sorry.' He sat down suddenly, leaned his head back and closed his eyes.

'God, but he's handsome!' Token Ware said reverently. 'And brave.'

Vidaury put his hand to his left shoulder, pressed it hard against his body. Blood oozed slowly between his fingers. Token Ware let out a stifled screech.

Pete Anglich looked down the room. The little Jap in the white coat had crept into the end of it, stood silently, a small huddled figure against the wall. Pete Anglich looked at Vidaury again. Very slowly, as though unwillingly, he said: 'Miss Ware has folks in 'Frisco. You can send her home, with a little present. That's natural – and open. She turned Waltz up to me. That's how I came into it. I told him you were wise and he came here to shut you up. Tough-guy stuff. The coppers will laugh at it, but they'll laugh in their cuffs. After all, they're getting publicity too. The phoney angle is out. Check?'

Vidaury opened his eyes, said faintly: 'You're – you're very decent about it. I won't forget.' His head lolled.

'He's fainted,' the girl cried.

'So he has,' Pete Anglich said. 'Give him a nice big kiss and he'll snap out of it. . . . And you'll have something to remember all your life.'

He ground his teeth, went to the phone, and lifted it.

Nevada Gas

I

Hugo Candless stood in the middle of the squash court bending his big body at the waist, holding the little black ball delicately between left thumb and forefinger. He dropped it near the service line and flicked at it with the long-handled racket.

The black ball hit the front wall a little less than halfway up, floated back in a high, lazy curve, skimmed just below the white ceiling and the lights behind wire protectors. It slid languidly down the back wall, never touching it enough to bounce out.

George Dial made a careless swing at it, whanged the end of his racket against the cement back wall. The ball fell dead.

He said: 'That's the story, chief. Twenty-one fourteen. You're just too good for me.'

George Dial was tall, dark, handsome, Hollywoodish. He was brown and lean, and had a hard, outdoor look. Everything about him was hard except his full, soft lips and his large, cow-like eyes.

'Yeah. I always was too good for you,' Hugo Candless chortled.

He leaned far back from his thick waist and laughed with his mouth wide open. Sweat glistened on his chest and belly. He was naked except for blue shorts, white wool socks and heavy sneakers with crêpe soles. He had grey hair and a broad moon face with a small nose and mouth, sharp twinkly eyes.

'Want another lickin'?' he asked.

'Not unless I have to.'

Hugo Candless scowled. 'Oke,' he said shortly. He stuck his racket under his arm and got an oilskin pouch out of his shorts, took a cigarette and a match from it. He lit the cigarette with a flourish and threw the match into the middle of the court, where somebody else would have to pick it up.

He threw the door of the squash court open and paraded down the corridor to the locker room with his chest out. Dial walked behind him silently; catlike, soft-footed, with a lithe grace. They went to the showers.

Candless sang in the showers, covered his big body with thick suds, showered dead-cold after the hot, and liked it. He rubbed himself dry with immense leisure, took another towel and stalked out of the shower room yelling for the attendant to bring ice and ginger ale.

A negro in a stiff white coat came hurrying with a tray. Candless signed the check with a flourish, unlocked his big double locker and planked a bottle of Johnny Walker on the round green table that stood in the locker aisle.

The attendant mixed drinks carefully, two of them, said: 'Yes, suh, Mista Candless,' and went away palming a quarter.

George Dial, already fully dressed in smart grey flannels, came around the corner and lifted one of the drinks.

'Through for the day, chief?' He looked at the ceiling light through his drink, with tight eyes.

'Guess so,' Candless said largely. 'Guess I'll go home and give the little woman a treat.' He gave Dial a swift, sidewise glance from his little eyes.

'Mind if I don't ride home with you?' Dial asked carelessly.

'With me it's okay. It's tough on Naomi,' Candless said unpleasantly.

Dial made a soft sound with his lips, shrugged, said: 'You like to burn people up, don't you, chief?'

Candless didn't answer, didn't look at him. Dial stood silent with his drink and watched the big man put on monogrammed satin underclothes, purple socks with grey clocks, a monogrammed silk shirt, a suit of tiny black and white checks that made him look as big as a barn.

By the time he got to his purple tie he was yelling for the negro to come and mix another drink.

Dial refused the second drink, nodded, went away softly along the matting between the tall green lockers.

Candless finished dressing, drank his second highball, locked his liquor away and put a fat brown cigar in his mouth. He had the negro light the cigar for him. He went off with a strut and several loud greetings here and there.

It seemed very quiet in the locker room after he went out. There were a few snickers.

It was raining outside the Delmar Club. The liveried doorman helped Hugo Candless on with his belted white raincoat and went out for his car. When he had it in front of the canopy he held an umbrella over Hugo across the strip of wooden matting to the kerb. The car was a royal blue Lincoln limousine, with buff striping. The licence number was 5A6.

The chauffeur, in a black raincoat turned up high around his ears, didn't look around. The doorman opened the door and Hugo Candless got in and sank heavily on the back seat.

' 'Night, Sam. Tell him to go on home.'

The doorman touched his cap, shut the door, and relayed the orders to the driver, who nodded without turning his head. The car moved off in the rain.

The rain came down slantingly and at the intersections sudden gusts blew it rattling against the glass of the limousine. The street corners were clotted with people trying to get across Sunset without being splashed. Hugo Candless grinned out at them, pityingly.

The car went out Sunset, through Sherman, then swung towards the hills. It began to go very fast. It was on a boulevard where traffic was thin now.

It was very hot in the car. The windows were all shut and the glass partition behind the driver's seat was shut all the way across. The smoke of Hugo's cigar was heavy and choking in the tonneau of the limousine.

Candless scowled and reached out to lower a window. The window lever didn't work. He tried the other side. That didn't work either. He began to get mad. He grabbed for the little telephone dingus to bawl his driver out. There wasn't any little telephone dingus.

The car turned sharply and began to go up a long straight hill with eucalyptus trees on one side and no houses. Candless felt something cold touch his spine, all the way up and down his spine. He bent forward and banged on the glass with his fist. The driver didn't turn his head. The car went very fast up the long dark hill road.

Hugo Candless grabbed viciously for the door handle. The doors didn't have any handles – either side. A sick, incredulous grin broke over Hugo's broad moon face.

The driver bent over to the right and reached for something with his gloved hand. There was a sudden sharp hissing noise. Hugo Candless began to smell the odour of almonds.

Very faint at first – very faint, and rather pleasant. The hissing noise went on. The smell of almonds got bitter and harsh and very deadly. Hugo Candless dropped his cigar and banged with all his strength on the glass of the nearest window. The glass didn't break.

The car was up in the hills now, beyond even the infrequent street lights of the residential sections.

Candless dropped back on the seat and lifted his foot to kick hard at the glass partition in front of him. The kick was never finished. His eyes no longer saw. His face twisted into a snarl and his head went back against the cushions, crushed down against his thick shoulders. His soft white felt hat was shapeless on his big square skull.

The driver looked back quickly, showing a lean, hawklike face for a brief instant. Then he bent to his right again and the hissing noise stopped.

He pulled over to the side of the deserted road, stopped the car, switched off all the lights. The rain made a dull noise pounding on the roof.

The driver got out in the rain and opened the rear door of the car, then backed away from it quickly, holding his nose.

He stood a little way off for a while and looked up and down the road.

In the back of the limousine Hugo Candless didn't move.

2

Francine Ley sat in a low red chair beside a small table on which there was an alabaster bowl. Smoke from the cigarette she had just discarded into the bowl floated up and made patterns in the still, warm air. Her hands were clasped behind her head and her smoke-blue eyes were lazy, inviting. She had dark auburn hair set in loose waves. There were bluish shadows in the troughs of the waves.

George Dial leaned over and kissed her on the lips, hard. His own lips were hot when he kissed her, and he shivered. The girl didn't move. She smiled up at him lazily when he straightened again.

In a thick, clogged voice Dial said: 'Listen, Francy. When do you ditch this gambler and let me set you up?'

Francine Ley shrugged, without taking her hands from behind her head. 'He's a square gambler, George,' she drawled. 'That's something nowadays and you don't have enough money.'

'I can get it.'

'How?' Her voice was low and husky. It moved George Dial like a 'cello.

'From Candless. I've got plenty on that bird.'

'As for instance?' Francine Ley suggested lazily.

Dial grinned softly down at her. He widened his eyes in a deliberately innocent expression. Francine Ley thought the whites of his eyes were tinged ever so faintly with some colour that was not white.

Dial flourished an unlighted cigarette. 'Plenty – like he sold out a tough boy from Reno last year. The tough boy's half-brother was under a murder rap here and Candless took twenty-five grand to get him off. He made a deal with the D.A. on another case and let the tough boy's brother go up.'

'And what did the tough boy do about all that?' Francine Ley asked gently.

'Nothing – yet. He thinks it was on the up and up, I guess. You can't always win.'

'But he might do plenty, if he knew,' Francine Ley said, nodding. 'Who was the tough boy, Georgie?'

Dial lowered his voice and leaned down over her again. 'I'm a sap to tell you this. A man named Zapparty. I've never met him.'

'And never want to – if you've got sense, Georgie. No, thanks. I'm not walking myself into any jam like that with you.'

Dial smiled lightly, showing even teeth in a dark, smooth face. 'Leave it to me, Francy. Just forget the whole thing except how I'm nuts about you.'

'Buy us a drink,' the girl said.

The room was a living-room in an hotel apartment. It was all red and white, with embassy decorations, too stiff. The white walls had red designs painted on them, the white venetian blinds were framed in white box drapes, there was a half-round red rug with a white border in front of the gas fire. There was a kidney-shaped white desk against one wall, between the windows.

Dial went over to the desk and poured Scotch into two glasses, added ice and charged water, carried the glasses back across the room to where a thin wisp of smoke still plumed upward from the alabaster bowl.

'Ditch that gambler,' Dial said, handing her a glass. 'He's the one will get you in a jam.'

She sipped the drink, nodded. Dial took the glass out of her hand, sipped from the same place on the rim, leaned over holding both glasses and kissed her on the lips again.

There were red curtains over a door to a short hallway. They were parted a few inches and a man's face appeared in the opening, cool grey eyes stared in thoughtfully at the kiss. The curtains fell together again without sound.

After a moment a door shut loudly and steps came along

the hallway. Johnny De Ruse came through the curtains into the room. By that time Dial was lighting his cigarette.

Johnny De Ruse was tall, lean, quiet, dressed in dark clothes dashingly cut. His cool grey eyes had fine laughter wrinkles at the corners. His thin mouth was delicate but not soft, and his long chin had a cleft in it.

Dial stared at him, made a vague motion with his hand. De Ruse walked over to the desk, without speaking, poured some whisky into a glass and drank it straight.

He stood a moment with his back to the room, tapping on the edge of the desk. Then he turned around, smiled faintly, said: ' 'Lo, people,' in a gentle, rather drawling voice and went out of the room through an inner door.

He was in a big overdecorated bedroom with twin beds. He went to a closet and got a tan calfskin suitcase out of it, opened it on the nearest bed. He began to rob the drawers of a highboy and put things in the suitcase, arranging them carefully, without haste. He whistled quietly through his teeth while he was doing it.

When the suitcase was packed he snapped it shut and lit a cigarette. He stood for a moment in the middle of the room, without moving. His grey eyes looked at the wall without seeing it.

After a little while he went back into the closet and came out with a small gun in a soft leather harness with two short straps. He pulled up the left leg of his trousers and strapped the holster on his leg. Then he picked up the suitcase and went back to the living-room.

Francine Ley's eyes narrowed swiftly when she saw the suit-case.

'Going some place?' she asked in her low, husky voice.

'Uh-huh. Where's Dial?'

'He had to leave.'

'That's too bad,' De Ruse said softly. He put the suitcase down on the floor and stood beside her, moving his cool grey eyes over the girl's face, up and down her slim body, from her ankles to her auburn head. 'That's too bad,' he said. 'I like to see him around. I'm kind of dull for you.'

'Maybe you are, Johnny.'

He bent to the suitcase, but straightened without touching it and said casually: 'Remember Mops Parisi? I saw him in town today.'

Her eyes widened and then almost shut. Her teeth clicked lightly. The line of her jawbone stood out very distinctly for a moment.

De Ruse kept moving his glance up and down her face and body.

'Going to do anything about it?' she asked.

'I thought of taking a trip,' De Ruse said. 'I'm not so scrappy as I was once.'

'A powder,' Francine Ley said softly. 'Where do we go?'

'Not a powder – a trip,' De Ruse said tonelessly. 'And not we – *me*. I'm going alone.'

She sat still, watching his face, not moving a muscle.

De Ruse reached inside his coat and got out a long wallet that opened like a book. He tossed a tight sheaf of bills into the girl's lap, put the wallet away. She didn't touch the bills.

'That'll hold you for longer than you'll need to find a new playmate,' he said, without expression. 'I wouldn't say I won't send you more, if you need it.'

She stood up slowly and the sheaf of bills slid down her skirt to the floor. She held her arms straight down at the sides, the hands clenched so that the tendons on the backs of them were sharp. Her eyes were as dull as slate.

'That means we're through, Johnny?'

He lifted his suitcase. She stepped in front of him swiftly, with two long steps. She put a hand against his coat. He stood quite still, smiling gently with his eyes, but not with his lips. The perfume of Shalimar twitched at his nostrils.

'You know what you are, Johnny?' Her husky voice was almost a lisp.

He waited.

'A pigeon, Johnny. A pigeon.'

He nodded slightly. 'Check. I called copper on Mops Parisi. I don't like the snatch racket, baby. I'd call copper on it any day. I might even get myself hurt blocking it. That's old stuff. Through?'

'You called copper on Mops Parisi and you don't think he knows it, but maybe he does. So you're running away from him. You're leaving me.'

'Maybe I'm just tired of you, baby.'

She put her head back and laughed sharply, almost with a wild note. De Ruse didn't budge.

'You're not a tough boy, Johnny. You're soft. George Dial is harder than you are. Gawd, how soft you are, Johnny!'

She stepped back, staring at his face. Some flicker of almost unbearable emotion came and went in her eyes.

'You're such a handsome pup, Johnny. Gawd, but you're handsome. It's too bad you're soft.'

De Ruse said gently, without moving: 'Not soft, baby – just a bit sentimental. I like to clock the ponies and play seven-card stud and mess around with little red cubes with white spots on them. I like games of chance, including women. But when I lose I don't get sore and I don't chisel. I just move on to the next table. Be seein' you.'

He stooped, hefted the suitcase, and walked around her. He went across the room and through the red curtains without looking back.

Francine Ley stared with stiff eyes at the floor.

3

Standing under the scalloped glass canopy of the side entrance to the Chatterton, De Ruse looked up and down Irolo, towards the flashing lights of Wilshire and towards the dark quiet end of the side street.

The rain fell softly, slantingly. A light drop blew in under the canopy and hit the red end of his cigarette with a sputter. He hefted the suitcase and went along Irolo towards his sedan.

It was parked almost at the next corner, a shiny black Packard with a little discreet chromium here and there.

He stopped and opened the door and a gun came up swiftly from inside the car. The gun prodded against his chest. A voice said sharply: 'Hold it! The mitts high, sweets!'

De Ruse saw the man dimly inside the car. A lean hawk-like face on which some reflected light fell without making it distinct. He felt a gun hard against his chest, hurting his breast-bone. Quick steps came up behind him and another gun prodded his back.

'Satisfied?' another voice inquired.

De Ruse dropped the suitcase, lifted his hands and put them against the top of the car.

'Okay,' he said wearily. 'What is it – a heist?'

A snarling laugh came from the man in the car. A hand smacked De Ruse's hips from behind.

'Back up – slow!'

De Ruse backed up, holding his hands very high in the air.

'Not so high, punk,' the man behind said dangerously. 'Just shoulder high.'

De Ruse lowered them. The man in the car got out, straightened. He put his gun against De Ruse's chest again, put out a long arm and unbuttoned De Ruse's overcoat. De Ruse leaned backwards. The hand belonging to the long arm explored his pockets, his armpits. A .38 in a spring holster ceased to make weight under his arm.

'Got one, Chuck. Anything your side?'

'Nothin' on the hip.'

The man in front stepped away and picked up the suitcase.

'March, sweets. We'll ride in our heap.'

They went farther along Irolo. A big Lincoln limousine loomed up, a blue car with a lighter stripe. The hawk-faced man opened the rear door.

'In.'

De Ruse got in listlessly, spitting his cigarette end into the wet darkness, as he stooped under the roof of the car. A faint smell assailed his nose, a smell that might have been overripe peaches or almonds. He got into the car.

'In beside him, Chuck.'

'Listen. Let's all ride up front. I can handle — '

'Nix. In beside him, Chuck,' the hawk-faced one snapped.

Chuck growled, got into the back seat beside De Ruse. The other man slammed the door hard. His lean face showed through the closed window in a sardonic grin. Then he went around to the driver's seat and started the car, tooled it away from the kerb.

De Ruse wrinkled his nose, sniffing at the queer smell.

They spun at the corner, went east on Eighth to Normandie, north on Normandie across Wilshire, across other streets, up over a steep hill and down the other side to Melrose. The big Lincoln slid through the light rain without a whisper. Chuck sat in the corner, held his gun on his knee, scowled. Street lights showed a square, arrogant, red face, a face that was not at ease.

The back of the driver's head was motionless beyond the glass partition. They passed Sunset and Hollywood, turned east on Franklin, swung north to Los Feliz and down Los Feliz towards the river bed.

Cars coming up the hill threw sudden brief glares of white light into the interior of the Lincoln. De Ruse tensed, waited. At the next pair of lights that shot squarely into the car he bent over swiftly and jerked up the left leg of his trousers. He was back against the cushions before the blinding light was gone.

Chuck hadn't moved, hadn't noticed movement.

Down at the bottom of the hill, at the intersection of Riverside Drive, a whole phalanx of cars surged towards them as a light changed. De Ruse waited, timed the impact of the headlights. His body stooped briefly, his hand swooped down, snatched the small gun from the leg holster.

He leaned back once more, the gun against the bulk of his left thigh, concealed behind it from where Chuck sat.

The Lincoln shot over on to Riverside and passed the entrance to Griffith Park.

'Where we going, punk?' De Ruse asked casually.

'Save it,' Chuck snarled. 'You'll find out.'

'Not a stick-up, huh?'

'Save it,' Chuck snarled again.

'Mops Parisi's boys?' De Ruse asked thinly, slowly.

The red-faced gunman jerked, lifted the gun off his knee. 'I said – save it!'

De Ruse said: 'Sorry, punk.'

He turned the gun over his thigh, lined it swiftly, squeezed the trigger left-handed. The gun made a small flat sound – almost an unimportant sound.

Chuck yelled and his hand jerked wildly. The gun kicked out of it and fell on the floor of the car. His left hand raced for his right shoulder.

De Ruse shifted the little Mauser to his right hand and put it deep into Chuck's side.

'Steady boy, steady. Keep your hands out of trouble. Now – kick that cannon over this way – fast!'

Chuck kicked the big automatic along the floor of the car. De Ruse reached down for it swiftly, got it. The lean-faced driver jerked a look back and the car swerved, then straightened again.

De Ruse hefted the big gun. The Mauser was too light for a cosh. He slammed Chuck hard on the side of the head. Chuck groaned, sagged forward, clawing.

'The gas!' he bleated. 'The gas! He'll turn on the gas!'

De Ruse hit him again, harder. Chuck was a tumbled heap on the floor of the car.

The Lincoln swung off Riverside, over a short bridge and a bridle path, down a narrow dirt road that split a golf course. It went into darkness and among trees. It went fast, rocketed from side to side, as if the driver wanted it to do just that.

De Ruse steadied himself, felt for the door handle. There wasn't any door handle. His lips curled and he smashed at a window with the gun. The heavy glass was like a wall of stone.

The hawk-faced man leaned over and there was a hissing

sound. Then there was a sudden sharp increase of intensity of the smell of almonds.

De Ruse tore a handkerchief out of his pocket and pressed it to his nose. The driver had straightened again now and was driving hunched over, trying to keep his head down.

De Ruse held the muzzle of the big gun close to the glass partition behind the driver's head, who ducked sidewise. He squeezed lead four times quickly, shutting his eyes and turning his head away, like a nervous woman.

No glass flew. When he looked again there was a jagged round hole in the glass and the windshield in a line with it was starred but not broken.

He slammed the gun at the edges of the hole and managed to knock a piece of glass loose. He was getting the gas now, through the handkerchief. His head felt like a balloon. His vision waved and wandered.

The hawk-faced driver, crouched, wrenched the door open at his side, swung the wheel of the car the opposite way and jumped clear.

The car tore over a low embankment, looped a little and smacked sidewise against a tree. The body twisted enough for one of the rear doors to spring open.

De Ruse went through the door in a headlong dive. Soft earth smacked him, knocked some of the wind out of him. Then his lungs breathed clean air. He rolled up on his stomach and elbows, kept his head down, his gun hand up.

The hawk-faced man was on his knees a dozen yards away. De Ruse watched him drag a gun out of his pocket and lift it.

Chuck's gun pulsed and roared in De Ruse's hand until it was empty.

The hawk-faced man folded down slowly and his body merged with the dark shadows and the wet ground. Cars went by distantly on Riverside Drive. Rain dripped off the trees. The Griffith Park beacon turned in the thick sky. The rest was darkness and silence.

De Ruse took a deep breath and got up on his feet. He dropped the empty gun, took a small flash out of his overcoat pocket and pulled his overcoat up against his nose and mouth, pressing the thick cloth hard against his face. He went to the car, switched off the lights and threw the beam of the flash into the driver's compartment. He leaned in quickly and turned a petcock on a copper cylinder like a fire extinguisher. The hissing noise of the gas stopped.

He went over to the hawk-faced man. He was dead. There was some loose money, currency and silver in his pockets, cigarettes, a folder of matches from the Club Egypt, no wallet, a couple of extra clips of cartridges, De Ruse's .38. De Ruse put the last back where it belonged and straightened from the sprawled body.

He looked across the darkness of the Los Angeles riverbed towards the lights of Glendale. In the middle distance a green neon sign far from any other light winked on and off: Club Egypt.

De Ruse smiled quietly to himself, and went back to the Lincoln. He dragged Chuck's body out on to the wet ground. Chuck's red face was blue now, under the beam of the small flash. His open eyes held an empty stare. His chest didn't move. De Ruse put the flash down and went through some more pockets.

He found the usual things a man carries, including a wallet showing a driver's licence issued to Charles Le Grand, Hotel Metropole, Los Angeles. He found more Club Egypt matches and a tabbed hotel key marked 809, Hotel Metropole.

He put the key in his pocket, slammed the sprung door of the Lincoln, got in under the wheel. The motor caught. He backed the car away from the tree with a wrench of broken fender metal, swung it around slowly over the soft earth and got it back again on the road.

When he reached Riverside again he turned the lights on and drove back to Hollywood. He put the car under some pepper trees in front of a big brick apartment house on Kenmore, half a block north of Hollywood Boulevard, locked the ignition and lifted out his suitcase.

Light from the entrance of the apartment house rested on the front licence plate as he walked away. He wondered why gunmen would use a car with plate numbers reading 5A6, almost a privilege number.

In a drugstore he phoned for a taxi. The taxi took him back to the Chatterton.

4

The apartment was empty. The smell of Shalimar and cigarette smoke lingered on the warm air, as if someone had been there not long before. De Ruse pushed into the bedroom, looked at clothes in two closets, articles on a dresser, then went back to the red and white living-room and mixed himself a stiff highball.

He put the night latch on the outside door and carried his drink into the bedroom, stripped off his muddy clothes and put on another suit of sombre material but dandified cut. He sipped his drink while he knotted a black four-in-hand in the opening of a soft white linen shirt.

He stabbed the barrel of the little Mauser, reassembled it, and added a shell to the small clip, slipped the gun back into the leg holster. Then he washed his hands and took his drink to the telephone.

The first number he called was the *Chronicle*. He asked for the City Room, Werner.

A drawly voice dripped over the wire: 'Werner talkin'. Go ahead. Kid me.'

De Ruse said: 'This is John De Ruse, Claude. Look up California Licence 5A6 on your list for me.'

'Must be a bloody politician,' the drawly voice said, and went away.

De Ruse sat motionless, looking at a fluted white pillar in the corner. It had a red and white bowl of red and white artificial roses on top of it. He wrinkled his nose at it disgustedly.

Werner's voice came back on the wire: '1930 Lincoln limousine registered to Hugo Candless, Casa de Oro Apartments, 2942 Clearwater Street, West Hollywood.'

De Ruse said in a tone that meant nothing: 'That's the mouthpiece, isn't it?'

'Yeah. The big lip. Mister Take the Witness.' Werner's voice came down lower. 'Speaking to you, Johnny, and not for publication – a big crooked tub of guts that's not even smart; just been around long enough to know who's for sale. . . . Story in it?'

'Hell, no,' De Ruse said softly. 'He just sideswiped me and didn't stop.'

He hung up and finished his drink, stood up to mix another. Then he swept a telephone directory on to the white desk and looked up the number of the Casa de Oro. He dialled it. A switchboard operator told him Mr Hugo Candless was out of town.

'Give me his apartment,' De Ruse said.

A woman's cool voice answered the phone. 'Yes. This is Mrs Hugo Candless speaking. What is it, please?'

De Ruse said: 'I'm a client of Mr Candless, very anxious to get hold of him. Can you help me?'

'I'm very sorry,' the cool, almost lazy voice told him. 'My husband was called out of town quite suddenly. I don't even know where he went, though I expect to hear from him later this evening. He left his club —'

'What club was that?' De Ruse asked casually.

'The Delmar Club. I say he left there without coming home. If there is any message —'

De Ruse said: 'Thank you, Mrs Candless. Perhaps I may call you again later.'

He hung up, smiled slowly and grimly, sipped his fresh drink and looked up the number of the Hotel Metropole. He called it and asked for 'Mister Charles Le Grand in Room 809.'

'Six-o-nine,' the operator said casually. 'I'll connect you.' A moment later: 'There is no answer.'

De Ruse thanked her, took the tabbed key out of his pocket, looked at the number on it. The number was 809.

5

Sam, the doorman at the Delmar Club, leaned against the buff stone of the entrance and watched the traffic swish by on Sunset Boulevard. The headlights hurt his eyes. He was tired and he wanted to go home. He wanted a smoke and a big slug of gin. He wished the rain would stop. It was dead inside the club when it rained.

He straightened away from the wall and walked the length of the sidewalk canopy a couple of times, slapping together his big black hands in big white gloves. He tried to whistle the 'Skaters Waltz', couldn't get within a block of the tune, whistled 'Low Down Lady' instead. That didn't have any tune.

De Ruse came around the corner from Hudson Street and stood beside him near the wall.

'Hugo Candless inside?' he asked, not looking at Sam.

Sam clicked his teeth disapprovingly. 'He ain't.'

'Been in?'

'Ask at the desk 'side, please, mistah.'

De Ruse took gloved hands out of his pocket and began to roll a five-dollar bill around his left forefinger.

'What do they know that you don't know?'

Sam grinned slowly, watched the bill being wound tightly around the gloved finger.

'That's a fac', boss. Yeah – he was in. Comes most every day.'

'What time he leave?'

'He leave 'bout six-thirty, Ah reckon.'

'Drive his blue Lincoln limousine?'

'Shuah. Only he don't drive it hisself. What for you ask?'

'It was raining then,' De Ruse said calmly. 'Raining pretty hard. Maybe it wasn't the Lincoln.'

' 'Twas, too, the Lincoln,' Sam protested. 'Ain't I tucked him in? He never rides nothin' else.'

'Licence 5A6,' De Ruse bored on relentlessly.

'That's it,' Sam chortled. 'Just like a councilman's number that number is.'

'Know the driver?'

'Shuah — ' Sam began, and then stopped cold. He raked a black jaw with a white finger the size of a banana. 'Well, Ah'll be a big black slob if he ain't got hisself a new driver again. I ain't *know* that man, sure 'nough.'

De Ruse poked the rolled bill into Sam's big white paw. Sam grabbed it but his large eyes suddenly got suspicious.

'Say, for what you ask all of them questions, mistah man?'

De Ruse said: 'I paid my way, didn't I?'

He went back around the corner to Hudson and got into his black Packard sedan. He drove it out on to Sunset, then west on Sunset almost to Beverly Hills, then turned towards the foothills and began to peer at the signs on street corners. Clearwater Street ran along the flank of a hill and had a view of the entire city. The Casa de Oro, at the corner of Parkinson, was a tricky block of high-class bungalow apartments surrounded by an adobe wall with red tiles on top. It had a lobby in a separate building, a big private garage on Parkinson, opposite one length of the wall.

De Ruse parked across the street from the garage and sat looking through the wide window into a glassed-in office where an attendant in spotless white coveralls sat with his feet on the desk, reading a magazine and spitting over his shoulder at an invisible cuspidor.

De Ruse got out of the Packard, crossed the street farther up, came back and slipped into the garage without the attendant seeing him.

The cars were in four rows. Two rows backed against the white walls, two against each other in the middle. There were plenty of vacant stalls, but plenty of cars had gone to bed also. They were mostly big, expensive, closed models, with two or three flashy open jobs.

There was only one limousine. It had Licence No. 5A6.

It was a well-kept car, bright and shiny; royal blue with a buff trimming. De Ruse took a glove off and rested his hand on the radiator shell. Quite cold. He felt the tyres, looked at his fingers. A little fine dry dust adhered to the skin. There was no mud in the treads, just bone-dry dust.

He went back along the row of dark car bodies and leaned in the open door of the little office. After a moment the attendant looked up, almost with a start.

'Seen the Candless chauffeur around?' De Ruse asked him.

The man shook his head and spat deftly into a copper spittoon.

'Not since I came on – three o'clock.'

'Didn't he go down to the club for the old man?'

'Nope. I guess not. The big hack ain't been out. He always takes that.'

'Where does he hang his hat?'

'Who? Mattick? They got servants' quarters in back of the jungle. But I think I heard him say he parks at some hotel. Let's see — ' A brow got furrowed.

'The Metropole?' De Ruse suggested.

The garage man thought it over while De Ruse stared at the point of his chin.

'Yeah. I think that's it. I ain't just positive though. Mattick don't open up much.'

De Ruse thanked him and crossed the street and got into the Packard again. He drove downtown.

It was twenty-five minutes past nine when he got to the corner of Seventh and Spring, where the Metropole was.

It was an old hotel that had once been exclusive and was now steering a shaky course between a receivership and a bad name at Headquarters. It had too much oily dark wood panelling, too many chipped gilt mirrors. Too much smoke hung below its low beamed lobby ceiling and too many grifters bummed around in its worn leather rockers.

The blonde who looked after the big horseshoe cigar counter wasn't young any more and her eyes were cynical from standing off cheap dates. De Ruse leaned on the glass and pushed his hat back on his crisp black hair.

'Camels, honey,' he said in his low-pitched gambler's voice.

The girl smacked the pack in front of him, rang up fifteen cents and slipped the dime change under his elbow, with a faint smile. Her eyes said they liked him. She leaned opposite him and put her head near enough so that he could smell the perfume in her hair.

'Tell me something,' De Ruse said.

'What?' she asked softly.

'Find out who lives in eight-o-nine, without telling any answers to the clerk.'

The blonde looked disappointed. 'Why don't you ask him yourself, mister?'

'I'm too shy,' De Ruse said.

'Yes, you are!'

She went to her telephone and talked into it with languid grace, came back to De Ruse.

'Name of Mattick. Mean anything?'

'Guess not,' De Ruse said. 'Thanks a lot. How do you like it in this nice hotel?'

'Who said it was a nice hotel?'

De Ruse smiled, touched his hat, strolled away. Her eyes looked after him sadly. She leaned her sharp elbows on the counter and cupped her chin in her hands to stare after him.

De Ruse crossed the lobby and went up three steps and got into an open-cage elevator that started with a lurch.

'Eight,' he said, and leaned against the cage with his hands in his pockets.

Eight was as high as the Metropole went. De Ruse followed a long corridor that smelled of varnish. A turn at the end brought him face to face with 809. He knocked on the dark wood panel. Nobody answered. He bent over, looked through an empty keyhole, knocked again.

Then he took the tabbed key out of his pocket and unlocked the door and went in.

Windows were shut in two walls. The air reeked of whisky. Lights were on in the ceiling. There was a wide brass bed, a dark bureau, a couple of brown leather rockers, a stiff-looking desk with a flat brown quart of Four Roses on it, nearly empty, without a cap. De Ruse sniffed it and set his hips against the edge of the desk, let his eyes prowl the room.

His glance traversed from the dark bureau across the bed and the wall with the door in it to another door behind which light showed. He crossed to that and opened it.

The man lay on his face, on the yellowish brown wood-stone floor of the bathroom. Blood on the floor looked sticky and black. Two soggy patches on the back of the man's head were the points from which rivulets of dark red had run down the side of his neck to the floor. The blood had stopped flowing a long time ago.

De Ruse slipped a glove off and stooped to hold two fingers against the place where an artery would beat. He shook his head and put his hand back into his glove.

He left the bathroom, shut the door and went to open one of the windows. He leaned out, breathing clean rain-wet air, looking down along slants of thin rain into the dark slit of an alley.

After a little while he shut the window again, switched off the light in the bathroom, took a DO NOT DISTURB sign out of the top bureau drawer, doused the ceiling lights, and went out.

He hung the sign on the knob and went back along the corridor to the elevators and left the Hotel Metropole.

6

Francine Ley hummed low down in her throat as she went along the silent corridor of the Chatterton. She hummed unsteadily without knowing what she was humming, and her left hand with its cherry-red fingernails held a green velvet cape from slipping down off her shoulders. There was a wrapped bottle under her other arm.

She unlocked the door, pushed it open and stopped, with a

quick frown. She stood still, remembering, trying to remember. She was still a little tight.

She had left the lights on, that was it. They were off now.
Could be the maid service, of course. She went on in, fumbled
through the red curtains into the living-room.

The glow from the heater prowled across the red and white
rug and touched shiny black things with a ruddy gleam. The
shiny black things were shoes. They didn't move.

Francine Ley said: 'Oh – oh,' in a sick voice. The hand holding the cape almost tore into her neck with its long, beautifully
moulded nails.

Something clicked and light glowed in a lamp beside an easy
chair. De Ruse sat in the chair, looking at her woodenly.

He had his coat and hat on. His eyes were shrouded, far away,
filled with a remote brooding.

He said: 'Been out, Francy?'

She sat down slowly on the edge of a half-round settee, put
the bottle down beside her.

'I got tight,' she said. 'Thought I'd better eat. Then I thought
I'd get tight again.' She patted the bottle.

De Ruse said: 'I think your friend Dial's boss has been
snatched.' He said it casually, as if it was of no importance
to him.

Francine Ley opened her mouth slowly and as she opened it
all the prettiness went out of her face. Her face became a blank
haggard mask on which rouge burned violently. Her mouth
looked as if it wanted to scream.

After a while it closed again and her face got pretty again and
her voice, from far off, said: 'Would it do any good to say I
don't know what you're talking about?'

De Ruse didn't change his wooden expression. He said:
'When I went down to the street from here a couple of hoods
jumped me. One of them was stashed in the car. Of course they
could have spotted me somewhere else – followed me here.'

'They did,' Francine Ley said breathlessly. 'They did,
Johnny.'

His long chin moved an inch. 'They piled me into a big Lincoln, a limousine. It was quite a car. It had heavy glass that didn't break easily and no door handles and it was all shut up tight. In the front seat it had a tank of Nevada gas, cyanide, which the guy driving could turn into the back part without getting it himself. They took me out Griffith Park-way, towards the Club Egypt. That's that joint on county land, near the airport.' He paused, rubbed the end of one eyebrow, went on: 'They overlooked the Mauser I sometimes wear on my leg. The driver crashed the car and I got loose.'

He spread his hands and looked down at them. A faint metallic smile showed at the corners of his lips.

Francine Ley said: 'I didn't have anything to do with it, Johnny.' Her voice was as dead as the summer before last.

De Ruse said: 'The guy that rode in the car before I did probably didn't have a gun. He was Hugo Candless. The car was a ringer for his car – same model, same paint job, same plates– but it wasn't his car. Somebody took a lot of trouble. Candless left the Delmar Club in the wrong car about six-thirty. His wife says he's out of town. I talked to her an hour ago. His car hasn't been out of the garage since noon. . . . Maybe his wife knows he's snatched by now, maybe not.'

Francine Ley's nails clawed at her skirt. Her lips shook.

De Ruse went on calmly, tonelessly: 'Somebody gunned the Candless chauffeur in a downtown hotel tonight or this afternoon. The cops haven't found it yet. Somebody took a lot of trouble, Francy. You wouldn't want to be in on that kind of a set-up, would you, precious?'

Francine Ley bent her head forward and stared at the floor. She said thickly: 'I need a drink. What I had is dying in me. I feel awful.'

De Ruse stood up and went to the white desk. He drained a bottle into a glass and brought it across to her. He stood in front of her, holding the glass out of her reach.

'I only get tough once in a while, baby, but when I get tough I'm not so easy to stop, if I say it myself. If you know anything about all this, now would be a good time to spill it.'

He handed her the glass. She gulped the whisky and a little more light came into her smoke-blue eyes. She said slowly: 'I don't know anything about it, Johnny. Not in the way you mean. But George Dial made me a love-nest proposition to-night and he told me he could get money out of Candless by threatening to spill a dirty trick Candless played on some tough boy from Reno.'

'Damn clever, these greasers,' De Ruse said. 'Reno's my town, baby. I know all the tough boys in Reno. Who was it?'

'Somebody named Zapparty.'

De Ruse said very softly: 'Zapparty is the name of the man who runs the Club Egypt.'

Francine Ley stood up suddenly and grabbed his arm. 'Stay out of it, Johnny! For Christ sake, can't you stay out of it for just this once?'

De Ruse shook his head, smiled delicately, lingeringly at her. Then he lifted her hand off his arm and stepped back.

'I had a ride in their gas car, baby, and I didn't like it. I smelled their Nevada gas. I left my lead in somebody's gun punk. That makes me call copper or get jammed up with the law. If somebody's snatched and I call copper, there'll be another kidnap victim bumped off, more likely than not. Zapparty's a tough boy from Reno and that could tie in with what Dial told you, and if Mops Parisi is playing with Zapparty, that could make a reason to pull me into it. Parisi loathes my guts.'

'You don't have to be a one-man riot squad, Johnny,' Francine Ley said desperately.

He kept on smiling, with tight lips and solemn eyes. 'There'll be two of us, baby. Get yourself a long coat. It's still raining a little.'

She goggled at him. Her outstretched hand, the one that had been on his arm, spread its fingers stiffly, bent back from the palm, straining back. Her voice was hollow with fear.

'Me, Johnny? . . . Oh, please, not . . . '

De Ruse said gently: 'Get that coat, honey. Make yourself

look nice. It might be the last time we'll go out together.'

She staggered past him. He touched her arm softly, held it a moment, said almost in a whisper:

'*You* didn't put the finger on me, did you, Francy?'

She looked back stonily at the pain in his eyes, made a hoarse sound under her breath and jerked her arm loose, went quickly into the bedroom.

After a moment the pain went out of De Ruse's eyes and the metallic smile came back to the corners of his lips.

7

De Ruse half closed his eyes and watched the croupier's fingers as they slid back across the table and rested on the edge. They were round, plump, tapering fingers, graceful fingers. De Ruse raised his head and looked at the croupier's face. He was a bald-headed man of no particular age, with quiet blue eyes. He had no hair on his head at all, not a single hair.

De Ruse looked down at the croupier's hands again. The right hand turned a little on the edge of the table. The buttons on the sleeve of the croupier's brown velvet coat – cut like a dinner coat – rested on the edge of the table. De Ruse smiled his thin metallic smile.

He had three blue chips on the red. On that play the ball stopped at black 2. The croupier paid off two of the four other men who were playing.

De Ruse pushed five blue chips forward and settled them on the red diamond. Then he turned his head to the left and watched a huskily built blond young man put three red chips on the zero.

De Ruse licked his lips and turned his head farther, looked towards the side of the rather small room. Francine Ley was sitting on a couch backed to the wall, with her head leaning against it.

'I think I've got it, baby,' De Ruse said to her. 'I think I've got it.'

Francine Ley blinked and lifted her head away from the wall.

She reached for a drink on a low round table in front of her.

She sipped the drink, looked at the floor, didn't answer.

De Ruse looked back at the blond man. The three other men had made bets. The croupier looked impatient and at the same time watchful.

De Ruse said: 'How come you always hit zero when I hit red, and double zero when I hit black?'

The blond young man smiled, shrugged, said nothing.

De Ruse put his hand down on the layout and said very softly: 'I asked you a question, mister.'

'Maybe I'm Jesse Livermore,' the blond young man grunted. 'I like to sell short.'

'What is this – slow motion?' one of the other men snapped.

'Make your plays, please, gentlemen,' the croupier said.

De Ruse looked at him, said: 'Let it go.'

The croupier spun the wheel left-handed, flicked the ball with the same hand the opposite way. His right hand rested on the edge of the table.

The ball stopped at black 28, next to zero. The blond man laughed. 'Close,' he said, 'close.'

De Ruse checked his chips, stacked them carefully. 'I'm down six grand,' he said. 'It's a little raw, but I guess there's money in it. Who runs this clip joint?'

The croupier smiled slowly and stared straight into De Ruse's eyes. He asked quietly: 'Did you say clip joint?'

De Ruse nodded. He didn't bother to answer.

'I thought you said clip joint,' the croupier said, and moved one foot, put weight on it.

Three of the men who had been playing picked their chips up quickly and went over to a small bar in the corner of the room. They ordered drinks and leaned their backs against the wall by the bar, watching De Ruse and the croupier. The blond man stayed put and smiled sarcastically at De Ruse.

'Tsk, tsk,' he said thoughtfully. 'Your manners.'

Francine Ley finished her drink and leaned her head back

against the wall again. Her eyes came down and watched De Ruse furtively, under the long lashes.

A panelled door opened after a moment and a very big man with a black moustache and very rough black eyebrows came in. The croupier moved his eyes to him, then to De Ruse, pointing with his glance.

'Yes, I thought you said clip joint,' he repeated tonelessly.

The big man drifted to De Ruse's elbow, touched him with his own elbow.

'Out,' he said impassively.

The blond man grinned and put his hands in the pockets of his dark grey suit. The big man didn't look at him.

De Ruse glanced across the layout at the croupier and said: 'I'll take back my six grand and call it a day.'

'Out,' the big man said wearily, jabbing his elbow into De Ruse's side.

The bald-headed croupier smiled politely.

'You,' the big man said to De Ruse, 'ain't goin' to get tough, are you?'

De Ruse looked at him with sarcastic surprise. 'Well, well, the bouncer,' he said softly. 'Take him, Nicky.'

The blond man took his right hand out of his pocket and swung it. The cosh looked black and shiny under the bright lights. It hit the big man on the back of the head with a soft thud. The big man clawed at De Ruse, who stepped away from him quickly and took a gun out from under his arm. The big man clawed at the edge of the roulette table and fell heavily on the floor.

Francine Ley stood up and made a strangled sound in her throat.

The blond man skipped sidewise, whirled and looked at the bartender. The bartender put his hands on top of the bar. The three men who had been playing roulette looked very interested, but they didn't move.

De Ruse said: 'The middle button on his right sleeve, Nicky. I think it's copper.'

'Yeah.' The blond man drifted around the end of the table putting the cosh back in his pocket. He went close to the croupier and took hold of the middle of three buttons on his right cuff, jerked it hard. At the second jerk it came away and a thin wire followed it out of the sleeve.

'Correct,' the blond man said casually, let the croupier's arm drop.

'I'll take my six grand now,' De Ruse said. 'Then we'll go talk to your boss.'

The croupier nodded slowly and reached for the rack of chips beside the roulette table.

The big man on the floor didn't move. The blond man put his right hand behind his hip and took a .45 automatic out from inside his waistband at the back.

He swung it in his hand, smiling pleasantly around the room.

8

They went along a balcony that looked down over the dining-room and the dance floor. The lisp of hot jazz came up to them from the lithe, swaying bodies of a high-yaller band. With the lisp of jazz came the smell of food and cigarette smoke and perspiration. The balcony was high and the scene down below had a patterned look, like an overhead camera shot.

The bald-headed croupier opened a door in the corner of the balcony and went through without looking back. The blond man De Ruse had called Nicky went after him. Then De Ruse and Francine Ley.

There was a short hall with a frosted light in the ceiling. The door at the end of that looked like painted metal. The croupier put a plump finger on the small push button at the side, rang it in a certain way. There was a buzzing noise like the sound of an electric door release. The croupier pushed on the edge and opened it.

Inside was a cheerful room, half den and half office. There was a grate fire and a green leather davenport at right angles to it, facing the door. A man sitting on the davenport put a newspaper down and looked up and his face suddenly got livid. He was a small man with a tight round head, a tight round dark face. He had little lightless black eyes like buttons of jet.

There was a big flat desk in the middle of the room and a very tall man stood at the end of it with a cocktail shaker in his hands. His head turned slowly and he looked over his shoulder at the four people who came into the room, while his hands continued to agitate the cocktail shaker in gentle rhythm. He had a cavernous face with sunken eyes, loose greyish skin, and close-cropped reddish hair without shine or parting. A thin crosscross scar like a German *Mensur* scar showed on his left cheek.

The tall man put the cocktail shaker down and turned his body around and stared at the croupier. The man on the davenport didn't move. There was a crouched tensity in his not moving.

The croupier said: 'I think it's a stick-up. But I couldn't help myself. They coshed Big George.'

The blond man smiled gaily and took his .45 out of his pocket. He pointed it at the floor.

'He thinks it's a stick-up,' he said. 'Wouldn't that positively slay you?'

De Ruse shut the heavy door. Francine Ley moved away from him, towards the side of the room away from the fire. He didn't look at her. The man on the davenport looked at her, looked at everybody.

De Ruse said quietly: 'The tall one is Zapparty. The little one is Mops Parisi.'

The blond man stepped to one side, leaving the croupier alone in the middle of the room. The .45 covered the man on the davenport.

'Sure, I'm Zapparty,' the tall man said. He looked at De Ruse curiously for a moment.

Then he turned his back and picked the cocktail shaker up again, took out the plug and filled a shallow glass. He drained the glass, wiped his lips with a sheer lawn handkerchief and tucked the handkerchief back into his breast pocket very carefully, so that three points showed.

De Ruse smiled his thin metallic smile and touched one end of his left eyebrow with his forefinger. His right hand was in his jacket pocket.

'Nicky and I put on a little act,' he said. 'That was so the boys outside would have something to talk about if the going got too noisy when we came in to see you.'

'It sounds interesting,' Zapparty agreed. 'What did you want to see me about?'

'About that gas car you take people for rides in,' De Ruse said.

The man on the davenport made a very sudden movement and his hand jumped off his leg as if something had stung it. The blond man said: 'No . . . or yes, if you'd rather, Mister Parisi. It's all a matter of taste.'

Parisi became motionless again. His hand dropped back to his short thick thigh.

Zapparty widened his deep eyes a little. 'Gas car?' His tone was of mild puzzlement.

De Ruse went forward into the middle of the room near the croupier. He stood balanced on the balls of his feet. His grey eyes had a sleepy glitter but his face was drawn and tired, not young.

He said: 'Maybe somebody just tossed it in your lap, Zapparty, but I don't think so. I'm talking about the blue Lincoln, Licence 5A6, with the tank of Nevada gas in front. You know, Zapparty, the stuff they use on killers in our state.'

Zapparty swallowed and his large Adam's apple moved in and out. He puffed his lips, then drew them back against his teeth, then puffed them again.

The man on the davenport laughed out loud, seemed to be enjoying himself.

A voice that came from no one in the room said sharply: 'Just drop that gat, blondie. The rest of you grab air.'

De Ruse looked up towards an opened panel in the wall

beyond the desk. A gun showed in the opening, and a hand, but no body or face. Light from the room lit up the hand and the gun.

The gun seemed to point directly at Francine Ley. De Ruse said: 'Okay,' quickly, and lifted his hands, empty.

The blond man said: 'That'll be Big George – all rested and ready to go.' He opened his hand and let the .45 thud to the floor in front of him.

Parisi stood up very swiftly from the davenport and took a gun from under his arm. Zapparty took a revolver out of the desk drawer, levelled it. He spoke towards the panel: 'Get out, and stay out.'

The panel clicked shut. Zapparty jerked his head at the bald-headed croupier, who had not seemed to move a muscle since he came into the room.

'Back on the job, Louis. Keep the chin up.'

The croupier nodded and turned and went out of the room, closing the door carefully behind him.

Francine Ley laughed foolishly. Her hand went up and pulled the collar of her wrap close around her throat, as if it was cold in the room. But there were no windows and it was very warm, from the fire.

Parisi made a whistling sound with his lips and teeth and went quickly to De Ruse and stuck the gun he was holding in De Ruse's face, pushing his head back. He felt in De Ruse's pockets with his left hand, took the Colt, felt under his arms, circled around him, touched his hips, came to the front again.

He stepped back a little and hit De Ruse on the cheek with the flat of one gun. De Ruse stood perfectly still except that his head jerked a little when the hard metal hit his face.

Parisi hit him again the same place. Blood began to run down De Ruse's cheek from the cheekbone, lazily. His head sagged a little and his knees gave way. He went down slowly, leaned with his left hand on the floor, shaking his head. His body was crouched, his legs doubled under him. His right hand dangled loosely beside his left foot.

Zapparty said: 'All right, Mops. Don't get blood-hungry. We want words out of these people.'

Francine Ley laughed again, rather foolishly. She swayed along the wall, holding one hand up against it.

Parisi breathed hard and backed away from De Ruse with a happy smile on his round swart face.

'I been waitin' a long time for this,' he said.

When he was about six feet from De Ruse something small and darkly glistening seemed to slide out of the left leg of De Ruse's trousers into his hand. There was a sharp, snapping explosion, a tiny orange-green flame down on the floor.

Parisi's head jerked back. A round hole appeared under his chin. It got large and red almost instantly. His hands opened laxly and the two guns fell out of them. His body began to sway. He fell heavily.

Zapparty said: 'Holy Christ!' and jerked up his revolver.

Francine Ley screamed flatly and hurled herself at him – clawing, kicking, shrilling.

The revolver went off twice with a heavy crash. Two slugs plunked into a wall. Plaster rattled.

Francine Ley slid down to the floor, on her hands and knees. A long slim leg sprawled out from under her dress.

The blond man, down on one knee with his .45 in his hand again, rasped: 'She's got the bastard's gun!'

Zapparty stood with his hands empty, a terrible expression on his face. There was a long red scratch on the back of his right hand. His revolver lay on the floor beside Francine Ley. His horrified eyes looked down at it unbelievingly.

Parisi coughed once on the floor and after that was still.

De Ruse got up on his feet. The little Mauser looked like a toy in his hand. His voice seemed to come from far away, saying: 'Watch that panel, Nicky. . . .'

There was no sound outside the room, no sound anywhere. Zapparty stood at the end of the desk, frozen, ghastly.

De Ruse bent down and touched Francine Ley's shoulder. 'All right, baby?'

She drew her legs under her and got up, stood looking down at Parisi. Her body shook with a nervous chill.

'I'm sorry, baby,' De Ruse said softly beside her. 'I guess I had a wrong idea about you.'

He took a handkerchief out of his pocket and moistened it with his lips, then rubbed his left cheek lightly and looked at blood on the handkerchief.

Nicky said: 'I guess Big George went to sleep again. I was a sap not to blast at him.'

De Ruse nodded a little, and said:

'Yeah. The whole play was lousy. Where's your hat and coat, Mister Zapparty? We'd like to have you go riding with us.'

9

In the shadows under the pepper trees De Ruse said: 'There it is, Nicky. Over there. Nobody's bothered it. Better take a look around.'

The blond man got out from under the wheel of the Packard and went off under the trees. He stood a little while on the same side of the street as the Packard, then he slipped across to where the big Lincoln was parked in front of the brick apartment house on North Kenmore.

De Ruse leaned forward across the back of the front seat and pinched Francine Ley's cheek. 'You're going home now, baby – with this bus. I'll see you later.'

'Johnny' – she clutched at his arm – 'what are you going to do? For Pete's sake, can't you stop having fun for tonight?'

'Not yet, baby. Mister Zapparty wants to tell us things. I figure a little ride in that gas car will pep him up. Anyway, I need it for evidence.'

He looked sidewise at Zapparty in the corner of the back seat. Zapparty made a harsh sound in his throat and stared in front of him with a shadowed face.

Nicky came back across the road, stood with one foot on the running board.

'No keys,' he said. 'Got 'em?'

De Ruse said: 'Sure.' He took keys out of his pocket and handed them to Nicky. Nicky went around to Zapparty's side of the car and opened the door.

'Out, mister.'

Zapparty got out stiffly, stood in the soft, slanting rain, his mouth working. De Ruse got out after him.

'Take it away, baby.'

Francine Ley slid along the seat under the steering wheel of the Packard and pushed the starter. The motor caught with a soft whirr.

'So long, baby,' De Ruse said gently. 'Get my slippers warmed for me. And do me a big favour, honey. Don't phone anyone.'

The Packard went off along the dark street, under the big pepper trees. De Ruse watched it turn a corner. He prodded Zapparty with his elbow.

'Let's go. You're going to ride in the back of your gas car. We can't feed you much gas on account of the hole in the glass, but you'll like the smell of it. We'll go off in the country somewhere. We've got all night to play with you.'

'I guess you know this is a snatch,' Zapparty said harshly.

'Don't I love to think it,' De Ruse purred.

They went across the street, three men walking together without haste. Nicky opened the good rear door of the Lincoln. Zapparty got into it. Nicky banged the door shut, got under the wheel and fitted the ignition key in the lock. De Ruse got in beside him and sat with his legs straddling the tank of gas.

The whole car still smelled of the gas.

Nicky started the car, turned it in the middle of the block and drove north to Franklin, back over Los Feliz towards Glendale. After a little while Zapparty leaned forward and banged on the glass. De Ruse put his ear to the hole in the glass behind Nicky's head.

Zapparty's harsh voice said: 'Stone house – Castle Road – in the La Crescenta flood area.'

'Geez, but he's a softy,' Nicky grunted, his eyes on the road ahead.

De Ruse nodded, said thoughtfully: 'There's more to it than that. With Parisi dead he'd clam up unless he figured he had an out.'

Nicky said: 'Me, I'd rather take a beating and keep my chin buttoned. Light me a pill, Johnny.'

De Ruse lit two cigarettes and passed one to the blond man. He glanced back at Zapparty's long body in the corner of the car. Passing light touched up his taut face, made the shadows on it look very deep.

The big car slid noiselessly through Glendale and up the grade towards Montrose. From Montrose over to the Sunland highway and across that into the almost deserted flood area of La Crescenta.

They found Castle Road and followed it towards the mountains. In a few minutes they came to the stone house.

It stood back from the road, across a wide space which might once have been lawn but which was now packed sand, small stones and a few large boulders. The road made a square turn just before they came to it. Beyond it the road ended in a clean edge of concrete chewed off by the flood of New Year's Day, 1934.

Beyond this edge was the main wash of the flood. Bushes grew in it and there were many huge stones. On the very edge a tree grew with half its roots in the air eight feet above the bed of the wash.

Nicky stopped the car and turned off the lights and took a big nickelled flash out of the car pocket. He handed it to De Ruse.

De Ruse got out of the car and stood for a moment with his hand on the open door, holding the flash. He took a gun out of his overcoat pocket and held it down at his side.

'Looks like a stall,' he said. 'I don't think there's anything stirring here.'

He glanced in at Zapparty, smiled sharply and walked off across the ridges of sand, towards the house. The front door stood half open, wedged that way by sand. De Ruse went towards the corner of the house, keeping out of line with the door as well as he could. He went along the side wall, looking at boarded-up windows behind which there was no trace of light.

At the back of the house was what had been a chicken house. A piece of rusted junk in a squashed garage was all that remained of the family sedan. The back door was nailed up like the windows. De Ruse stood silent in the rain, wondering why the front door was open. Then he remembered that there had been another flood a few months before, not such a bad one. There might have been enough water to break open the door on the side towards the mountains.

Two stucco houses, both abandoned, loomed on the adjoining lots. Farther away from the wash, on a bit of higher ground, there was a lighted window. It was the only light anywhere in the range of De Ruse's vision.

He went back to the front of the house and slipped through the open door, stood inside it and listened. After quite a long time he snapped the flash on.

The house didn't smell like a house. It smelled like out of doors. There was nothing in the front room but sand, a few pieces of smashed furniture, some marks on the walls, above the dark line of the flood water, where pictures had hung.

De Ruse went through a short hall into a kitchen that had a hole in the floor where the sink had been and a rusty gas stove stuck in the hole. From the kitchen he went into a bedroom. He had not heard any whisper of sound in the house so far.

The bedroom was square and dark. A carpet stiff with old mud was plastered to the floor. There was a metal bed with a rusted spring, and a waterstained mattress over part of the spring.

Feet stuck out from under the bed.

They were large feet in walnut brown brogues, with purple socks above them. The socks had grey clocks down the sides. Above the socks were trousers of black and white check.

De Ruse stood very still and played the flash down on the

feet. He made a soft sucking sound with his lips. He stood like that for a couple of minutes, without moving at all. Then he stood the flash on the floor, on its end, so that the light it shot against the ceiling was reflected down to make dim light all over the room.

He took hold of the mattress and pulled it off the bed. He reached down and touched one of the hands of the man who was under the bed. The hand was ice cold. He took hold of the ankles and pulled, but the man was large and heavy.

It was easier to move the bed from over him.

10

Zapparty leaned his head back against the upholstery and shut his eyes and turned his head away a little. His eyes were shut very tight and he tried to turn his head far enough so that the light from the big flash wouldn't shine through his eyelids.

Nicky held the flash close to his face and snapped it on, off again, on, off again, monotonously, in a kind of rhythm.

De Ruse stood with one foot on the running board by the open door and looked off through the rain. On the edge of the murky horizon an airplane beacon flashed weakly.

Nicky said carelessly: 'You never know what'll get a guy. I saw one break once because a cop held his fingernail against the dimple in his chin.'

De Ruse laughed under his breath. 'This one is tough,' he said. 'You'll have to think of something better than a flash-light.'

Nicky snapped the flash on, off, on, off. 'I could,' he said, 'but I don't want to get my hands dirty.'

After a little while Zapparty raised his hands in front of him and let them fall slowly and began to talk. He talked in a low monotonous voice, keeping his eyes shut against the flash.

'Parisi worked the snatch. I didn't know anything about it until it was done. Parisi muscled in on me about a month ago, with a couple of tough boys to back him up. He had found out somehow that Candless beat me out of twenty-five grand to defend my half-brother on a murder rap, then sold the kid out. I didn't tell Parisi that. I didn't know he knew until tonight.

'He came into the club about seven or a little after and said: "We've got a friend of yours, Hugo Candless. It's a hundred-grand job, a quick turnover. All you have to do is help spread the pay-off across the tables here, get it mixed up with a bunch of other money. You have to do that because we give you a cut – and because the caper is right up your alley, if anything goes sour." That's about all. Parisi sat around then and chewed his fingers and waited for his boys. He got pretty jumpy when they didn't show. He went out once to make a phone call from a beer parlour.'

De Ruse drew on a cigarette he held cupped inside a hand.

He said: 'Who fingered the job, and how did you know Candless was up here?'

Zapparty said: 'Mops told me. But I didn't know he was dead.'

Nicky laughed and snapped the flash several times quickly.

De Ruse said: 'Hold it steady for a minute.'

Nicky held the beam steady on Zapparty's white face. Zapparty moved his lips in and out. He opened his eyes once. They were blind eyes, like the eyes of a dead fish.

Nicky said: 'It's damn cold up here. What do we do with his nibs?'

De Ruse said: 'We'll take him into the house and tie him to Candless. They can keep each other warm. We'll come up again in the morning and see if he's got any fresh ideas.'

Zapparty shuddered. The gleam of something like a tear showed in the corner of his nearest eye. After a moment of silence he said: 'Okay. I planned the whole thing. The gas car was my idea. I didn't want the money. I wanted Candless, and I wanted him dead. My kid brother was hanged in Quentin a week ago Friday.'

There was a little silence. Nicky said something under his breath. De Ruse didn't move or make a sound.

Zapparty went on: 'Mattick, the Candless driver, was in

on it. He hated Candless. He was supposed to drive the ringer car to make everything look good and then take a powder. But he lapped up too much corn getting set for the job and Parisi got leery of him, had him knocked off. Another boy drove the car. It was raining and that helped.'

De Ruse said: 'Better – but still not all of it, Zapparty.'

Zapparty shrugged quickly, slightly opened his eyes against the flash, almost grinned.

'What the hell do you want? Jam on both sides?'

De Ruse said: 'I want a finger put on the bird that had me grabbed. . . . Let it go. I'll do it myself.'

He took his foot off the running board and snapped his butt away in the darkness. He slammed the car door shut, got in the front. Nicky put the flash away and slid around under the wheel, started the engine.

De Ruse said: 'Somewhere where I can phone for a cab, Nicky. Then you take this riding for another hour and then call Francy. I'll have a word for you there.'

The blond man shook his head slowly from side to side. 'You're a good pal, Johnny, and I like you. But this has gone far enough this way. I'm taking it down to Headquarters. Don't forget I've got a private dick licence under my old shirts at home.'

De Ruse said: 'Give me an hour, Nicky. Just an hour.'

The car slid down the hill and crossed the Sunland Highway, started down another hill towards Montrose. After a while Nicky said: 'Check.'

11

It was twelve minutes past one by the stamping clock on the end of the desk in the lobby of the Casa de Oro. The lobby was antique Spanish, with black and red Indian rugs, nail-studded chairs with leather cushions and leather tassels on the corners of the cushions; the grey-green olive wood doors were fitted with clumsy wrought-iron strap hinges.

A thin, dapper clerk with a waxed blond moustache and a

blond pompadour leaned on the desk and looked at the clock and yawned, tapping his teeth with the backs of his bright fingernails.

The door opened from the street and De Ruse came in. He took off his hat and shook it, put it on again and yanked the brim down. His eyes looked slowly around the deserted lobby and he went to the desk, slapped a gloved palm on it.

'What's the number of the Hugo Candless bungalow?' he asked.

The clerk looked annoyed. He glanced at the clock, at De Ruse's face, back at the clock. He smiled superciliously, spoke with a slight accent.

'Twelve C. Do you wish to be announced – at this hour?'

De Ruse said: 'No.'

He turned away from the desk and went towards a large door with a diamond of glass in it. It looked like the door of a very high-class privy.

As he put his hand out to the door a bell rang sharply behind him.

De Ruse looked back over his shoulder, turned and went back to the desk. The clerk took his hand away from the bell, rather quickly.

His voice was cold, sarcastic, insolent, saying: 'It's not that kind of apartment house, if you please.'

Two patches above De Ruse's cheekbones got a dusky red. He leaned across the counter and took hold of the braided lapel of the clerk's jacket, pulled the man's chest against the edge of the desk.

'What was that crack, nance?'

The clerk paled but managed to bang his bell again with a flailing hand.

A pudgy man in a baggy suit and a seal-brown toupee came around the corner of the desk, put out a plump finger and said: 'Hey.'

De Ruse let the clerk go. He looked expressionlessly at cigar ash on the front of the pudgy man's coat.

The pudgy man said: 'I'm the house man. You gotta see me if you want to get tough.'

De Ruse said: 'You speak my language. Come over in the corner.'

They went over in the corner and sat down beside a palm. The pudgy man yawned amiably and lifted the edge of his toupee and scratched under it.

'I'm Kuvalick,' he said. 'Times I could bop that Swiss myself. What's the beef?'

De Ruse said: 'Are you a guy that can stay clammed?'

'No. I like to talk. It's all the fun I get around this dude ranch.' Kuvalick got half of a cigar out of a pocket and burned his nose lighting it.

De Ruse said: 'This is one time you stay clammed.'

He reached inside his coat, got his wallet out, took out two tens. He rolled them around his forefinger, then slipped them off in a tube and tucked the tube into the outside pocket of the pudgy man's coat.

Kuvalick blinked, but didn't say anything.

De Ruse said: 'There's a man in the Candless apartment named George Dial. His car's outside, and that's where he would be. I want to see him and I don't want to send a name in. You can take me in and stay with me.'

The pudgy man said cautiously: 'It's kind of late. Maybe he's in bed.'

'If he is, he's in the wrong bed,' De Ruse said. 'He ought to get up.'

The pudgy man stood up. 'I don't like what I'm thinkin', but I like your tens,' he said. 'I'll go in and see if they're up. You stay put.'

De Ruse nodded. Kuvalick went along the wall and slipped through a door in the corner. The clumsy square butt of a hip holster showed under the back of his coat as he walked. The clerk looked after him, then looked contemptuously towards De Ruse and got out a nail file.

Ten minutes went by, fifteen. Kuvalick didn't come back.

De Ruse stood up suddenly, scowled and marched towards the door in the corner. The clerk at the desk stiffened, and his eyes went to the telephone on the desk, but he didn't touch it.

De Ruse went through the door and found himself under a roofed gallery. Rain dripped softly off the slanting tiles of the roof. He went along a patio the middle of which was an oblong pool framed in a mosaic of gaily coloured tiles. At the end of that, other patios branched off. There was a window light at the far end of the one to the left. He went towards it, at a venture, and when he came close to it made out the number 12C on the door.

He went up two flat steps and punched a bell that rang in the distance. Nothing happened. In a little while he rang again, then tried the door. It was locked. Somewhere inside he thought he heard a faint muffled thumping sound.

He stood in the rain a moment, then went around the corner of the bungalow, down a narrow, very wet passage to the back. He tried the service door; locked also. De Ruse swore, took his gun out from under his arm, held his hat against the glass panel of the service door and smashed the pane with the butt of the gun. Glass fell tinkling lightly inside.

He put the gun away, straightened his hat on his head and reached in through the broken pane to unlock the door.

The kitchen was large and bright with black and yellow tiling, looked as if it was used mostly for mixing drinks. Two bottles of Haig and Haig, a bottle of Hennessy, three or four kinds of fancy cordial bottles stood on the tiled drainboard. A short hall with a closed door led to the living-room. There was a grand piano in the corner with a lamp lit beside it. Another lamp on a low table with drinks and glasses. A wood fire was dying on the hearth.

The thumping noise got louder.

De Ruse went across the living-room and through a door framed in a valance into another hallway, thence into a beautifully panelled bedroom. The thumping noise came from a closet. De Ruse opened the door of the closet and saw a man.

He was sitting on the floor with his back in a forest of dresses on hangers. A towel was tied around his face. Another held his ankles together. His wrists were tied behind him. He was a very bald man, as bald as the croupier at the Club Egypt.

De Ruse stared down at him harshly, then suddenly grinned, bent and cut him loose.

The man spat a washcloth out of his mouth, swore hoarsely and dived into the clothes at the back of the closet. He came up with something furry clutched in his hand, straightened it out, and put it on his hairless head.

That made him Kuvalick, the house dick.

He got up still swearing and backed away from De Ruse, with a stiff alert grin on his fat face. His right hand shot to his hip holster.

De Ruse spread his hands, said: 'Tell it,' and sat down in a small chintz-covered slipper chair.

Kuvalick stared at him quietly for a moment, then took his hand away from his gun.

'There's lights,' he said, 'so I push the buzzer. A tall dark guy opens. I seen him around here a lot. That's Dial. I say to him there's a guy outside in the lobby wants to see him hush-hush, won't give a name.'

'That made you a sap,' De Ruse commented dryly.

'Not yet, but soon,' Kuvalick grinned, and spat a shred of cloth out of his mouth. 'I describe you. *That* makes me a sap. He smiled kind of funny and asks me to come in a minute. I go in past him and he shuts the door and sticks a gun in my kidney. He says: "Did you say he wore all dark clothes?" I say: "Yes. And what's that gat for?" He says: "Does he have grey eyes and sort of crinkly black hair and is he hard around the teeth?" I say: "Yes, you bastard, and what's the gat for?"

'He says: "For this," and lets me have it on the back of the head. I go down, groggy, but not out. Then the Candless broad comes out from a doorway and they tie me up and shove me in the closet and that's that. I hear them fussin' around for a little while and then I hear silence. That's all until you ring the bell.'

De Ruse smiled lazily, pleasantly. His whole body was lax in the chair. His manner had become indolent and unhurried.

'They faded,' he said softly. 'They got tipped off. I don't think that was very bright.'

Kuvalick said: 'I'm an old Wells Fargo dick and I can stand a shock. What they been up to?'

'What kind of woman is Mrs Candless?'

'Dark, a looker. Sex-hungry, as the fellow says. Kind of worn and tight. They get a new chauffeur every three months. There's a couple guys in the Casa she likes too. I guess there's this gigolo that bopped me.'

De Ruse looked at his watch, nodded, leaned forward to get up. 'I guess it's about time for some law. Got any friends downtown you'd like to give a snatch story to?'

A voice said: 'Not quite yet.'

George Dial came quickly into the room from the hallway and stood quietly inside it with a long, thin, silenced automatic in his hand. His eyes were bright and mad, but his lemon-coloured finger was very steady on the trigger of the small gun.

'We didn't fade,' he said. 'We weren't quite ready. But it might not have been a bad idea – for you two.'

Kuvalick's pudgy hand swept for his hip holster.

The small automatic with the black tube on it made two flat dull sounds.

A puff of dust jumped from the front of Kuvalick's coat. His hands jerked sharply away from the sides and his small eyes snapped very wide open, like seeds bursting from a pod. He fell heavily on his side against the wall, lay quite still on his left side, with his eyes half open and his back against the wall. His toupee was tipped over rakishly.

De Ruse looked at him swiftly, looked back at Dial. No emotion showed in his face, not even excitement.

He said: 'You're a crazy fool, Dial. That kills your last

chance. You could have bluffed it out. But that's not your only mistake.'

Dial said calmly: 'No. I see that now. I shouldn't have sent the boys after you. I did that just for the hell of it. That comes of not being a professional.'

De Ruse nodded slightly, looked at Dial almost with friendliness. 'Just for the fun of it – who tipped you off the game had gone smash?'

'Francy – and she took her damn time about it,' Dial said savagely. 'I'm leaving, so I won't be able to thank her for a while.'

'Not ever,' De Ruse said. 'You won't get out of the state. You won't ever touch a nickel of the big boy's money. Not you or your sidekicks or your woman. The cops are getting the story – right now.'

Dial said: 'We'll get clear. We have enough to tour on, Johnny. So long.'

Dial's face tightened and his hand jerked up, with the gun in it. De Ruse half closed his eyes, braced himself for the shock. The little gun didn't go off. There was a rustle behind Dial and a tall dark woman in a grey fur coat slid into the room. A small hat was balanced on dark hair knotted on the nape of her neck. She was pretty, in a thin, haggard sort of way. The lip rouge on her mouth was as black as soot; there was no colour in her cheeks.

She had a cool lazy voice that didn't match with her taut expression. 'Who is Francy?' she asked coldly.

De Ruse opened his eyes wide and his body got stiff in the chair and his right hand began to slide up towards his chest.

'Francy is my girl friend,' he said. 'Mister Dial has been trying to get her away from me. But that's all right. He's a handsome lad and ought to be able to pick his spots.'

The tall woman's face suddenly became dark and wild and furious. She grabbed fiercely at Dial's arm, the one that held the gun.

De Ruse snatched for his shoulder holster, got his .38 loose.

But it wasn't his gun that went off. It wasn't the silenced automatic in Dial's hand. It was a huge frontier Colt with an eight-inch barrel and a boom like an exploding bomb. It went off from the floor, from beside Kuvalick's right hip, where Kuvalick's plump hand held it.

It went off just once. Dial was thrown back against the wall as if by a giant hand. His head crashed against the wall and instantly his darkly handsome face was a mask of blood.

He fell laxly down the wall and the little automatic with the black tube on it fell in front of him. The dark woman dived for it, down on her hands and knees in front of Dial's sprawled body.

She got it, began to bring it up. Her face was convulsed, her lips were drawn back over thin wolfish teeth that shimmered.

Kuvalick's voice said: 'I'm a tough guy. I used to be a Wells Fargo dick.'

His great cannon slammed again. A shrill scream was torn from the woman's lips. Her body was flung against Dial's. Her eyes opened and shut, opened and shut. Her face got white and vacant.

'Shoulder shot. She's okay,' Kuvalick said, and got up on his feet. He jerked open his coat and patted his chest.

'Bullet-proof vest,' he said proudly. 'But I thought I'd better lie quiet for a while or he'd popped me in the face.'

12

Francine Ley yawned and stretched out a long green pyjama clad leg and looked at a slim green slipper on her bare foot. She yawned again, got up and walked nervously across the room to the kidney-shaped desk. She poured a drink, drank it quickly, with a sharp nervous shudder. Her face was drawn and tired, her eyes hollow; there were dark smudges under her eyes.

She looked at the tiny watch on her wrist. It was almost four o'clock in the morning. Still with her wrist up she whirled at a sound, put her back to the desk and began to breathe very quickly, pantingly.

De Ruse came in through the red curtains. He stopped and looked at her without expression, then slowly took off his hat and overcoat and dropped them on a chair. He took off his suit coat and his tan shoulder harness and walked over to the drinks.

He sniffed at a glass, filled it a third full of whisky, put it down in a gulp.

'So you had to tip the louse off,' he said sombrely, looking down into the empty glass he held.

Francine Ley said: 'Yes. I had to phone him. What happened?'

'You had to phone the louse,' De Ruse said in exactly the same tone. 'You knew damn well he was mixed up in it. You'd rather he got loose, even if he cooled me off doing it.'

'You're all right, Johnny?' she asked softly, tiredly.

De Ruse didn't speak, didn't look at her. He put the glass down slowly and poured some more whisky into it, added charged water, looked around for some ice. Not finding any he began to sip the drink, with his eyes on the white top of the desk.

Francine Ley said: 'There isn't a guy in the world that doesn't rate a start on you, Johnny. It wouldn't do him any good, but he'd have to have it, if I knew him.'

De Ruse said slowly: 'That's swell. Only I'm not quite that good. I'd be a stiff right now except for a comic hotel dick that wears a Buntline Special and a bullet-proof vest to work.'

After a little while Francine Ley said: 'Do you want me to blow?'

De Ruse looked at her quickly, looked away again. He put his glass down and walked away from the desk. Over his shoulder he said, 'Not so long as you keep on telling me the truth.'

He sat down in a deep chair and leaned his elbows on the arms of it, cupped his face in his hands. Francine Ley watched him for a moment, then went over and sat on an arm of the chair. She pulled his head back gently until it was against the back of the chair. She began to stroke his forehead.

De Ruse closed his eyes. His body became loose and relaxed. His voice began to sound sleepy.

'You saved my life over at the Club Egypt maybe. I guess that gave you the right to let handsome have a shot at me.'

Francine Ley stroked his head, without speaking.

'Handsome is dead,' De Ruse went on. 'The peeper shot his face off.'

Francine Ley's hand stopped. In a moment it began again, stroking his head.

'The Candless frau was in on it. Seems she's a hot number. She wanted Hugo's dough, and she wanted all the men in the world except Hugo. Thank heaven *she* didn't get bumped. She talked plenty. So did Zapparty.'

'Yes, honey,' Francine Ley said quietly.

De Ruse yawned. 'Candless is dead. He was dead before we started. They never wanted him anything else but dead. Parisi didn't care one way or the other, as long as he got paid.'

Francine Ley said: 'Yes, honey.'

'Tell you the rest in the morning,' De Ruse said thickly. 'I guess Nicky and I are all square with the law. . . . Let's go to Reno, get married . . . I'm sick of this tomcat life. . . . Get me 'nother drink, baby.'

Francine Ley didn't move except to draw her fingers softly and soothingly across his forehead and back over his temples. De Ruse moved lower in the chair. His head rolled to one side.

'Yes, honey.'

'Don't call me honey,' De Ruse said thickly. 'Just call me pigeon.'

When he was quite asleep she got off the arm of the chair and went and sat down near him. She sat very still and watched him, her face cupped in her long delicate hands with the cherry-coloured nails.

Spanish Blood

I

Big John Masters was large, fat, oily. He had sleek blue jowls and very thick fingers on which the knuckles were dimples. His brown hair was combed straight back from his forehead and he wore a wine-coloured suit with patch pockets, a wine-coloured tie, a tan silk shirt. There was a lot of red and gold band around the thick brown cigar between his lips.

He wrinkled his nose, peeped at his hole card again, tried not to grin. He said: 'Hit me again, Dave – and don't hit me with the City Hall.'

A four and a deuce showed. Dave Aage looked at them solemnly across the table, looked down at his own hand. He was very tall and thin, with a long bony face, and hair the colour of wet sand. He held the deck flat on the palm of his hand, turned the top card slowly, and flicked it across the table. It was the queen of spades.

Big John Masters opened his mouth wide, waved his cigar about, chuckled.

'Pay me, Dave. For once a lady was right.' He turned his hole card with a flourish. A five.

Dave Aage smiled politely, didn't move. A muted telephone bell rang close to him, behind long silk drapes that bordered the very high lancet windows. He took a cigarette out of his mouth and laid it carefully on the edge of a tray on a tabouret beside the card table, reached behind the curtain for the phone.

He spoke into the cup with a cool, almost whispering voice, then listened for a long time. Nothing changed in his greenish eyes, no flicker of emotion showed on his narrow face. Masters squirmed, bit hard on his cigar.

After a long time Aage said: 'Okay, you'll hear from us.' He pronged the instrument and put it back behind the curtain.

He picked his cigarette up, pulled the lobe of his ear. Masters swore. 'What's eating you, for pete's sake? Gimme ten bucks.'

Aage smiled dryly and leaned back. He reached for a drink, sipped it, put it down, spoke around his cigarette. All his movements were slow, thoughtful, almost absent-minded. He said: 'Are we a couple of smart guys, John?'

'Yeah. We own the town. But it don't help my blackjack game any.'

'It's just two months to election, isn't it, John?'

Masters scowled at him, fished in his pocket for a fresh cigar, jammed it into his mouth.

'So what?'

'Suppose something happened to our toughest opposition. Right now. Would that be a good idea, or not?'

'Huh?' Masters raised eyebrows so thick that his whole face seemed to have to work to push them up. He thought for a moment, sourly. 'It would be lousy – if they didn't catch the guy pronto. Hell, the voters would figure we hired it done.'

'You're talking about murder, John,' Aage said patiently, 'I didn't say anything about murder.'

Masters lowered his eyebrows and pulled at coarse black hair that grew out of his nose.

'Well, spit it out!'

Aage smiled, blew a smoke ring, watched it float off and come apart in frail wisps.

'I just had a phone call,' he said very softly. 'Donegan Marr is dead.'

Masters moved slowly. His whole body moved slowly towards the card table, leaned far over it. When his body couldn't go any farther his chin came out until his jaw muscles stood out like thick wires.

'Huh?' he said thickly. 'Huh?'

Aage nodded, calm as ice. 'But you were right about murder, John. It *was* murder. Just half an hour ago, or so. In his office. They don't know who did it – yet.'

Masters shrugged heavily and leaned back. He looked around him with a stupid expression. Very suddenly he began to laugh. His laughter bellowed and roared around the little turretlike room where the two men sat, overflowed into an enormous living-room beyond, echoed back and forth through a maze of heavy dark furniture, enough standing lamps to light a boulevard, a double row of oil paintings in massive gold frames.

Aage sat silent. He rubbed his cigarette out, slowly in the tray until there was nothing of the fire left but a thick dark smudge. He dusted his bony fingers together and waited.

Masters stopped laughing as abruptly as he had begun. The room was very still. Masters looked tired. He mopped his big face.

'We got to do something, Dave,' he said quietly. 'I almost forgot. We got to break this fast. It's dynamite.'

Aage reached behind the curtain again and brought the phone out, pushed it across the table over the scattered cards.

'Well – we know how, don't we?' he said calmly.

A cunning light shone in Big John Masters' muddy brown eyes. He licked his lips, reached a big hand for the phone.

'Yeah,' he said purringly, 'we do, Dave. We do at that, by — !'

He dialled with a thick finger that would hardly go into the holes.

2

Donegan Marr's face looked cool, neat, poised, even then. He was dressed in soft grey flannels and his hair was the same soft grey colour as his suit, brushed back from a ruddy, youngish face. The skin was pale on the frontal bones where the hair would fall when he stood up. The rest of the skin was tanned.

He was lying back in a padded blue office chair. A cigar had gone out in a tray with a bronze greyhound on its rim. His left hand dangled beside the chair and his right hand held a gun loosely on the desk top. The polished nails glittered in sunlight from the big closed window behind him.

Blood had soaked the left side of his vest, made the grey flannel almost black. He was quite dead, had been dead for some time.

A tall man, very brown and slender and silent, leaned against a brown mahogany filing cabinet and looked fixedly at the dead man. His hands were in the pockets of a neat blue serge suit. There was a straw hat on the back of his head. But there was nothing casual about his eyes or his tight, straight mouth.

A big sandy-haired man was groping around on the blue rug. He said thickly, stooped over: 'No shells, Sam.'

The dark man didn't move, didn't answer. The other stood up, yawned, looked at the man in the chair.

'Hell! This one will stink. Two months to election. Boy, is this a smack in the puss for somebody.'

The dark man said slowly: 'We went to school together. We used to be buddies. We carried the torch for the same girl. He won, but we stayed good friends, all three of us. He was always a great kid. . . . Maybe a shade too smart.'

The sandy-haired man walked around the room without touching anything. He bent over and sniffed at the gun on the desk, shook his head, said: 'Not used – this one.' He wrinkled his nose, sniffed at the air. 'Air conditioned. The three top floors. Sound-proofed too. High-grade stuff. They tell me this whole building is electric-welded. Not a rivet in it. Ever hear that, Sam?'

The dark man shook his head slowly.

'Wonder where the help was,' the sandy-haired man went on. 'A big shot like him would have more than one girl.'

The dark man shook his head again. 'That's all, I guess. She was out to lunch. He was a lone wolf, Pete. Sharp as a weasel. In a few more years he'd have taken the town over.'

The sandy-haired man was behind the desk now, almost leaning over the dead man's shoulder. He was looking down at a leather-backed appointment pad with buff leaves. He said slowly: 'Somebody named Imlay was due here at twelve-fifteen. Only date on the pad.'

He glanced at a cheap watch on his wrist. 'One-thirty. Long gone. Who's Imlay? . . . Say, wait a minute! There's an assistant D.A. named Imlay. He's running for judge on the Masters-Aage ticket. D'you figure — '

There was a sharp knock on the door. The office was so long that the two men had to think a moment before they placed which of the three doors it was. Then the sandy-haired man went towards the most distant of them, saying over his shoulder: 'M.E.'s man maybe. Leak this to your favourite newshawk and you're out a job. Am I right?'

The dark man didn't answer. He moved slowly to the desk, leaned forward a little, spoke softly to the dead man.

'Good-bye, Donny. Just let it all go. I'll take care of it. I'll take care of Belle.'

The door at the end of the office opened and a brisk man with a bag came in, trotted down the blue carpet and put his bag on the desk. The sandy-haired man shut the door against a bulge of faces. He strolled back to the desk.

The brisk man cocked his head on one side, examining the corpse. 'Two of them,' he muttered. 'Look like about .32's – hard slugs. Close to the heart but not touching. He must have died pretty soon. Maybe a minute or two.'

The dark man made a disgusted sound and walked to the window, stood with his back to the room, looking out, at the tops of high buildings and a warm blue sky. The sandy-haired man watched the examiner lift a dead eyelid. He said: 'Wish the powder guy would get here. I wanta use the phone. This Imlay — '

The dark man turned his head slightly, with a dull smile. 'Use it. This isn't going to be any mystery.'

'Oh, I don't know,' the M.E.'s man said, flexing a wrist, then holding the back of his hand against the skin of the dead man's face. 'Might not be so damn political as you think, Delaguerra. He's a good-looking stiff.'

The sandy-haired man took hold of the phone gingerly, with a handkerchief, laid the receiver down, dialled, picked the receiver up with a handkerchief and put it to his ear.

After a moment he snapped his chin down, said: 'Pete Marcus. Wake the Inspector.' He yawned, waited again, then spoke in a different tone: 'Marcus and Delaguerra, Inspector, from Donegan Marr's office. No print or camera men here yet. . . . Huh? . . . Holding off till the Commissioner gets here? . . . Okay. . . . Yeah, he's here.'

The dark man turned. The man at the phone gestured at him. 'Take it, Spanish.'

Sam Delaguerra took the phone, ignoring the careful handkerchief, listened. His face got hard. He said quietly: 'Sure I knew him – but I didn't sleep with him. . . . Nobody's here but his secretary, a girl. She phoned the alarm in. There's a name on a pad – Imlay, a twelve-fifteen appointment. No, we haven't touched anything yet. . . . No. . . . Okay, right away.'

He hung up so slowly that the click of the instrument was barely audible. His hand stayed on it, then fell suddenly and heavily to his side. His voice was thick.

'I'm called off it, Pete. You're to hold it down until Commissioner Drew gets here. Nobody gets in. White, black or Cherokee Indian.'

'What you called in for?' the sandy-haired man yelped angrily.

'Don't know. It's an order,' Delaguerra said tonelessly.

The M.E.'s man stopped writing on a form pad to look curiously at Delaguerra, with a sharp, sidelong look.

Delaguerra crossed the office and went through the communicating door. There was a smaller office outside, partly partitioned off for a waiting room, with a group of leather chairs and a table with magazines. Inside a counter was a type-writer desk, a safe, some filing cabinets. A small dark girl sat at the desk with her head down on a wadded handkerchief. Her hat was crooked on her head. Her shoulders jerked and her thick sobs were like panting.

Delaguerra patted her shoulder. She looked up at him with a tear-bloated face, a twisted mouth. He smiled down at her questioning face, said gently: 'Did you call Mrs Marr yet?'

She nodded, speechless, shaken with rough sobs. He patted her shoulder again, stood a moment beside her, then went on out, with his mouth tight and a hard, dark glitter in his black eyes.

3

The big English house stood a long way back from the narrow, winding ribbon of concrete that was called De Neve Lane. The lawn had rather long grass with a curving path of stepping stones half hidden in it. There was a gable over the front door and ivy on the wall. Trees grew all around the house, close to it, made it a little dark and remote.

All the houses in De Neve Lane had that same calculated air of neglect. But the tall green hedge that hid the driveway and the garages was trimmed as carefully as a French poodle, and there was nothing dark or mysterious about the mass of yellow and flame-coloured gladioli that flared at the opposite end of the lawn.

Delaguerra got out of a tan-coloured Cadillac touring car that had no top. It was an old model, heavy and dirty. A taut canvas formed a deck over the back part of the car. He wore a white linen cap and dark glasses and had changed his blue serge for a grey cloth outing suit with a jerkin-style zipper jacket.

He didn't look very much like a cop. He hadn't looked very much like a cop in Donegan Marr's office. He walked slowly up the path of stepping stones, touched a brass knocker on the front door of the house, then didn't knock with it. He pushed a bell at the side, almost hidden by the ivy.

There was a long wait. It was very warm, very silent. Bees droned over the warm bright grass. There was the distant whirring of a lawn mower.

The door opened slowly and a black face looked out at him, a long, sad black face with tear streaks on its lavender face powder. The black face almost smiled, said haltingly: 'Hello there, Mistah Sam. It's sure good to see you.'

Delaguerra took his cap off, swung the dark glasses at his side. He said: 'Hello, Minnie. I'm sorry. I've got to see Mrs Marr.'

'Sure. Come right in, Mistah Sam.'

The maid stood aside and he went into a shadowy hall with a tile floor. 'No reporters yet?'

The girl shook her head slowly. Her warm brown eyes were stunned, doped with shock.

'Ain't been nobody yet. . . . She ain't been in long. She ain't said a word. She just stand there in that there sun room that ain't got no sun.'

Delaguerra nodded, said: 'Don't talk to anybody, Minnie. They're trying to keep this quiet for a while, out of the papers.'

'Ah sure won't, Mistah Sam. Not nohow.'

Delaguerra smiled at her, walked noiselessly on crêpe soles along the tiled hall to the back of the house, turned into another hall just like it at right angles. He knocked at a door. There was no answer. He turned the knob and went into a long narrow room that was dim in spite of many windows. Trees grew close to the windows, pressing their leaves against the glass. Some of the windows were masked by long cretonne drapes.

The tall girl in the middle of the room didn't look at him. She stood motionless, rigid. She stared at the windows. Her hands were tightly clenched at her sides.

She had red-brown hair that seemed to gather all the light there was and make a soft halo around her coldly beautiful face. She wore a sportily cut blue velvet ensemble with patch pockets. A white handkerchief with a blue border stuck out of the breast pocket, arranged carefully in points, like a foppish man's handkerchief.

Delaguerra waited, letting his eyes get used to the dimness. After a while the girl spoke through the silence, in a low, husky voice.

'Well . . . they got him, Sam. They got him at last. Was he so much hated?'

Delaguerra said softly: 'He was in a tough racket, Belle. I guess he played it as clean as he could, but he couldn't help but make enemies.'

She turned her head slowly and looked at him. Lights shifted in her hair. Gold glinted in it. Her eyes were vividly, startlingly blue. Her voice faltered a little, saying: 'Who killed him, Sam? Have they any ideas?'

Delaguerra nodded slowly, sat down in a wicker chair, swung his cap and glasses between his knees.

'Yeah. We think we know who did it. A man named Imlay, an assistant in the D.A.'s office.'

'My God!' the girl breathed. 'What's this rotten city coming to?'

Delaguerra went on tonelessly: 'It was like this – if you're sure you want to know . . . yet.'

'I do, Sam. His eyes stare at me from the wall, wherever I look. Asking me to do something. He was pretty swell to me, Sam. We had our troubles, of course, but . . . they didn't mean anything.'

Delaguerra said: 'This Imlay is running for judge with the backing of the Masters-Aage group. He's in the gay forties and it seems he's been playing house with a night-club number called Stella La Motte. Somehow, someway, photos were taken of them together, very drunk and undressed. Donny got the photos, Belle. They were found in his desk. According to his desk pad he had a date with Imlay at twelve-fifteen. We figure they had a row and Imlay beat him to the punch.'

'You found those photos, Sam?' the girl asked, very quietly.

He shook his head, smiled crookedly. 'No. If I had, I guess I might have ditched them. Commissioner Drew found them – after I was pulled off the investigation.'

Her head jerked at him. Her vivid blue eyes got wide. 'Pulled off the investigation? You – Donny's friend?'

'Yeah. Don't take it too big. I'm a cop, Belle. After all, I take orders.'

She didn't speak, didn't look at him any more. After a little while he said: 'I'd like to have the keys to your cabin at Puma Lake. I'm detailed to go up there and look around, see if there's any evidence. Donny had conferences there.'

Something changed in the girl's face. It got almost contemptuous. Her voice was empty. 'I'll get them. But you won't find anything there. If you're helping them to find dirt on Donny – so they can clear this Imlay person. . . .'

He smiled a little, shook his head slowly. His eyes were very deep, very sad.

'That's crazy talk, kid. I'd turn my badge in before I did that.'

'I see.' She walked past him to the door, went out of the room. He sat quite still while she was gone, looked at the wall with an empty stare. There was a hurt look on his face. He swore very softly, under his breath.

The girl came back, walked up to him and held her hand out. Something tinkled into his palm.

'The keys, copper.'

Delaguerra stood up, dropped the keys into a pocket. His face got wooden. Belle Marr went over to a table and her nails scratched harshly on a cloisonné box, getting a cigarette out of it. With her back turned she said: 'I don't think you'll have any luck, as I said. It's too bad you've only got blackmailing on him so far.'

Delaguerra breathed out slowly, stood a moment, then turned away. 'Okay,' he said softly. His voice was quite offhand now, as if it was a nice day, as if nobody had been killed.

At the door he turned again. 'I'll see you when I get back, Belle. Maybe you'll feel better.'

She didn't answer, didn't move. She held the unlighted cigarette rigidly in front of her mouth, close to it. After a moment Delaguerra went on: 'You ought to know how I feel about it. Donny and I were like brothers once. I – I heard you were not getting on so well with him . . . I'm glad as all hell that was wrong. But don't let yourself get too hard, Belle. There's nothing to be hard about – with me.'

He waited a few seconds, staring at her back. When she still didn't move or speak he went on out.

4

A narrow rocky road dropped down from the highway and ran along the flank of the hill above the lake. The tops of cabins showed here and there among the pines. An open shed was cut into the side of the hill. Delaguerra put his dusty Cadillac under it and climbed down a narrow path towards the water.

The lake was deep blue but very low. Two or three canoes drifted about on it and the chugging of an outboard motor sounded in the distance, around a bend. He went along between thick walls of undergrowth, walking on pine needles, turned around a stump and crossed a small rustic bridge to the Marr cabin.

It was built of half-round logs and had a wide porch on the lake side. It looked very lonely and empty. The spring that ran under the bridge curved around beside the house, and one end of the porch dropped down sheer to the big flat stones through which the water trickled. The stones would be covered when the water was high, in the spring.

Delaguerra went up wooden steps and took the keys out of his pocket, unlocked the heavy front door, then stood on the porch a little while and lit a cigarette before he went in. It was very still, very pleasant, very cool and clear after the heat of the city. A mountain bluejay sat on a stump and pecked at its wings. Somebody far out on the lake fooled with a ukelele. He went into the cabin.

He looked at some dusty antlers, a big rough table spattered with magazines, an old-fashioned battery-type radio, a box-shaped phonograph with a dishevelled pile of records beside it. There were tall glasses that hadn't been washed and a half-bottle of Scotch beside them, on a table near the big stone fireplace. A car went along the road up above and stopped somewhere not far off. Delaguerra frowned around, said: 'Stall,' under his breath, with a defeated feeling. There wasn't any sense in it. A man like Donegan Marr wouldn't leave anything that mattered in a mountain cabin.

He looked into a couple of bedrooms, one just a shake-down with a couple of cots, one better furnished, with a make-up bed, and a pair of women's gaudy pyjamas tossed across it. They didn't look quite like Belle Marr's.

At the back there was a small kitchen with a gasoline stove and a wood stove. He opened the back door with another key and stepped out on a small porch flush with the ground, near a big pile of cordwood and a double-bitted axe on a chopping block.

Then he saw the flies.

A wooden walk went down the side of the house to a wood-shed under it. A beam of sunlight had slipped through the trees and lay across the walk. In the sunlight there a clotted mass of flies festered on something brownish, sticky. The flies didn't want to move. Delaguerra bent down, then put his hand down and touched the sticky place, sniffed at his finger. His face got shocked and stiff.

There was another smaller patch of the brownish stuff farther on, in the shade, outside the door of the shed. He took the keys out of his pocket very quickly and found the one that unlocked the big padlock of the woodshed. He yanked the door open.

There was a big loose pile of cordwood inside. Not split wood – cordwood. Not stacked, just thrown in anyhow. Delaguerra began to toss the big rough pieces to one side.

After he had thrown a lot of it aside he was able to reach down and take hold of two cold stiff ankles in lisle socks and drag the dead man out into the light.

He was a slender man, neither tall nor short, in a well-cut basket-weave suit. His small neat shoes were polished, a little dust over the polish. He didn't have any face, much. It was broken to pulp by a terrific smash. The top of his head was split open and brains and blood were mixed in the thin greyish-brown hair.

Delaguerra straightened quickly and went back into the

house to where the half-bottle of Scotch stood on the table in the living-room. He uncorked it, drank from the neck, waited a moment, drank again.

He said: 'Phew!' out loud, and shivered as the whisky whipped at his nerves.

He went back to the woodshed, leaned down again as an automobile motor started up somewhere. He stiffened. The motor swelled in sound, then the sound faded and there was silence again. Delaguerra shrugged, went through the dead man's pockets. They were empty. One of them, with cleaner's marks on it probably, had been cut away. The tailor's label had been cut from the inside pocket of the coat, leaving ragged stitches.

The man was stiff. He might have been dead twenty-four hours, not more. The blood on his face had coagulated thickly but had not dried completely.

Delaguerra squatted beside him for a little while, looking at the bright glitter of Puma Lake, the distant flash of a paddle from a canoe. Then he went back into the woodshed and pawed around for a heavy block of wood with a great deal of blood on it, didn't find one. He went back into the house and out on the front porch, went to the end of the porch, stared down the drop, then at the big flat stones in the spring.

'Yeah,' he said softly.

There were flies clotted on two of the stones, a lot of flies. He hadn't noticed them before. The drop was about thirty feet, enough to smash a man's head open if he landed just right.

He sat down in one of the big rockers and smoked for several minutes without moving. His face was still with thought, his black eyes withdrawn and remote. There was a tight, hard smile, ever so faintly sardonic, at the corners of his mouth.

At the end of that he went silently back through the house and dragged the dead man into the woodshed again, covered him up loosely with the wood. He locked the woodshed, locked the house up, went back along the narrow, steep path to the road and to his car.

It was past six o'clock, but the sun was still bright as he drove off.

5

An old store counter served as bar in the roadside beerhouse. Three low stools stood against it. Delaguerra sat on the end one near the door, looked at the foamy inside of an empty beer glass. The bartender was a dark kid in overalls, with shy eyes and lank hair. He stuttered. He said: 'Sh-should I d-draw you another g-glass, mister?'

Delaguerra shook his head, stood up off the stool. 'Racket beer, sonny,' he said sadly. 'Tasteless as a roadhouse blonde.'

'P-portola B-brew, mister. Supposed to be the b-best.'

'Uh-huh. The worst. You use it, or you don't have a licence. So long, sonny.'

He went across to the screen door, looked out at the sunny highway on which the shadows were getting quite long. Beyond the concrete there was a gravelled space edged by a white fence of four-by-fours. There were two cars parked there: Delaguerra's old Cadillac and a dusty hard-bitten Ford. A tall, thin man in khaki whipcord stood beside the Cadillac, looking at it.

Delaguerra got a bulldog pipe out, filled it half full from a zipper pouch, lit it with slow care and flicked the match into the corner. Then he stiffened a little, looking out through the screen.

The tall, thin man was unsnapping the canvas that covered the back part of Delaguerra's car. He rolled part of it back, stood peering down in the space underneath.

Delaguerra opened the screen door softly and walked in long, loose strides across the concrete of the highway. His crêpe soles made sound on the gravel beyond, but the thin man didn't turn. Delaguerra came up beside him.

'Thought I noticed you behind me,' he said dully. 'What's the grift?'

The man turned without any haste. He had a long, sour face,

eyes the colour of seaweed. His coat was open, pushed back by a hand on a left hip. That showed a gun, worn butt to the front in a belt holster, cavalry style.

He looked Delaguerra up and down with a faint crooked smile.

'This your crate?'

'What do you think?'

The thin man pulled his coat back farther and showed a bronze badge on his pocket.

'I think I'm a Toluca County game warden, mister. I think this ain't deer-hunting time and it ain't ever deer-hunting time for does.'

Delaguerra lowered his eyes very slowly, looked into the back of his car, bending over to see past the canvas. The body of a young deer lay there on some junk, beside a rifle. The soft eyes of the dead animal, unglazed by death, seemed to look at him with a gentle reproach. There was dried blood on the doe's slender neck.

Delaguerra straightened, said gently: 'That's damn cute.'

'Got a hunting licence?'

'I don't hunt,' Delaguerra said.

'Wouldn't help much. I see you got a rifle.'

'I'm a cop.'

'Oh – cop, huh? Would you have a badge?'

'I would.'

Delaguerra reached into his breast pocket, got the badge out, rubbed it on his sleeve, held it in the palm of his hand. The thin game warden stared down at it, licking his lips.

'Detective-lieutenant, huh? City police.' His face got distant and lazy. 'Okay, Lieutenant. We'll ride about ten miles downgrade in your heap. I'll thumb a ride back to mine.'

Delaguerra put the badge away, knocked his pipe out carefully, stamped the embers into the gravel. He replaced the canvas loosely.

'Pinched?' he asked gravely.

'Pinched, Lieutenant.'

'Let's go.'

He got in under the wheel of the Cadillac. The thin warden went around the other side, got in beside him. Delaguerra started the car, backed around and started off down the smooth concrete of the highway. The valley was a deep haze in the distance. Beyond the haze other peaks were enormous on the skyline. Delaguerra coasted the big car easily, without haste. The two men stared straight before them without speaking.

After a long time Delaguerra said: 'I didn't know they had deer at Puma Lake. That's as far as I've been.'

'There's a reservation by there, Lieutenant,' the warden said calmly. He stared through the dusty windshield. 'Part of the Toluca County Forest – or wouldn't you know that?'

Delaguerra said: 'I guess I wouldn't know it. I never shot a deer in my life. Police work hasn't made me that tough.'

The warden grinned, said nothing. The highway went through a saddle, then the drop was on the right side of the highway. Little canyons began to open out into the hills on the left. Some of them had rough roads in them, half overgrown, with wheel tracks.

Delaguerra swung the big car hard and suddenly to the left, shot it into a cleared space of reddish earth and dry grass, slammed the brake on. The car skidded, swayed, ground to a lurching stop.

The warden was flung violently to the right, then forward against the windshield. He cursed, jerked up straight and threw his right hand across his body at the holstered gun.

Delaguerra took hold of a thin, hard wrist and twisted it sharply towards the man's body. The warden's face whitened behind the tan. His left hand fumbled at the holster, then relaxed. He spoke in a tight, hurt voice.

'Makin' it worse, copper. I got a phone tip at Salt Springs. Described your car, said where it was. Said there was a doe carcass in it. I — '

Delaguerra loosed the wrist, snapped the belt holster open and jerked the Colt out of it. He tossed the gun from the car.

'Get out, County! Thumb that ride you spoke of. What's the matter – can't you live on your salary any more? You planted it yourself, back at Puma Lake, you goddamn chiseller!'

The warden got out slowly, stood on the ground with his face blank, his jaw loose and slack.

'Tough guy,' he muttered. 'You'll be sorry for this, copper. I'll swear a complaint.'

Delaguerra slid across the seat, got out of the right-hand door. He stood close to the warden, said very slowly: 'Maybe I'm wrong, mister. Maybe you did get a call. Maybe you did.'

He swung the doe's body out of the car, laid it down on the ground, watching the warden. The thin man didn't move, didn't try to get near his gun lying on the grass a dozen feet away. His seaweed eyes were dull, very cold.

Delaguerra got back into the Cadillac, snapped the brake off, started the engine. He backed to the highway. The warden still didn't make a move.

The Cadillac leaped forward, shot down the grade, out of sight. When it was quite gone the warden picked his gun up and holstered it, dragged the doe behind some bushes, and started to walk back along the highway towards the crest of the grade.

6

The girl at the desk in the Kenworthy said: 'This man called you three times, Lieutenant, but he wouldn't give a number. A lady called twice. Wouldn't leave name or number.'

Delaguerra took three slips of paper from her, read the name 'Joey Chill' on them and the various times. He picked up a couple of letters, touched his cap to the desk girl, and got into the automatic elevator. He got off at four, walked down a narrow, quiet corridor, unlocked a door. Without switching on any lights he went across to a big french window, opened it wide, stood there looking at the thick dark sky, the flash of neon lights, the stabbing beams of headlamps on Ortega Boulevard, two blocks over.

He lit a cigarette and smoked half of it without moving. His

face in the dark was very long, very troubled. Finally he left
the window and went into a small bedroom, switched on a
table lamp and undressed to the skin. He got under the shower,
towelled himself, put on clean linen and went into the kitchen-
ette to mix a drink. He sipped that and smoked another
cigarette while he finished dressing. The telephone in the
living-room rang as he was strapping on his holster.

It was Belle Marr. Her voice was blurred and throaty, as if
she had been crying for hours.

'I'm so glad to get you, Sam. I – I didn't mean the way I
talked. I was shocked and confused, absolutely wild inside.
You knew that, didn't you, Sam?'

'Sure, kid,' Delaguerra said. 'Think nothing of it. Anyway
you were right. I just got back from Puma Lake and I think I
was just sent up there to get rid of me.'

'You're all I have now, Sam. You won't let them hurt you,
will you?'

'Who?'

'You know. I'm no fool, Sam. I know this was all a plot, a
vile political plot to get rid of him.'

Delaguerra held the phone very tight. His mouth felt stiff
and hard. For a moment he couldn't speak. Then he said: 'It
might be just what it looks like, Belle. A quarrel over those
pictures. After all, Donny had a right to tell a guy like that to get
off the ticket. That wasn't blackmail. . . . And he had a gun in
his hand, you know.'

'Come out and see me when you can, Sam.' Her voice
lingered with a spent emotion, a note of wistfulness.

He drummed on the desk, hesitated again, said: 'Sure. . . .
When was anybody at Puma Lake last, at the cabin?'

'I don't know. I haven't been there in a year. He went . . .
alone. Perhaps he met people there. I don't know.'

He said something vaguely, after a moment said good-bye
and hung up. He stared at the wall over the writing desk. There
was a fresh light in his eyes, a hard glint. His whole face was
tight, not doubtful any more.

He went back to the bedroom for his coat and straw hat. On the way out he picked up the three telephone slips with the name 'Joey Chill' on them, tore them into small pieces and burned the pieces in an ashtray.

7

Pete Marcus, the big, sandy-haired dick, sat sidewise at a small littered desk in a bare office in which there were two such desks, faced to opposite walls. The other desk was neat and tidy, had a green blotter with an onyx pen set, a small brass calendar and an abalone shell for an ashtray.

A round straw cushion that looked something like a target was propped upright in a straight chair by the window. Pete Marcus had a handful of bank pens in his left hand and he was flipping them at the cushion, like a Mexican knife thrower. He was doing it absently, without much skill.

The door opened and Delaguerra came in. He shut the door and leaned against it, looking woodenly at Marcus. The sandy-haired man creaked his chair around and tilted it back against the desk, scratched his chin with a broad thumbnail.

'Hi, Spanish. Nice trip? The Chief's yappin' for you.'

Delaguerra grunted, stuck a cigarette between his smooth brown lips.

'Were you in Marr's office when those photos were found, Pete?'

'Yeah, but I didn't find them. The Commish did. Why?'

'Did you see him find them?'

Marcus stared a moment, then said quietly, guardedly: 'He found them all right, Sam. He didn't plant them – if that's what you mean.'

Delaguerra nodded, shrugged. 'Anything on the slugs?'

'Yeah. Not .32s – .25s. A damn vest-pocket rod. Copper-nickel slugs. An automatic, though, and we didn't find any shells.'

'Imlay remembered those,' Delaguerra said evenly, 'but he left without the photos he killed for.'

Marcus lowered his feet to the floor and leaned forward, looking up past his tawny eyebrows.

'That could be. They give him a motive, but with the gun in Marr's hand they kind of knock a premeditation angle.'

'Good headwork, Pete.' Delaguerra walked over to the small window, stood looking out of it. After a moment Marcus said dully: 'You don't see me doin' any work, do you, Spanish?'

Delaguerra turned slowly, went over and stood close to Marcus, looking down at him.

'Don't be sore, kid. You're my partner, and I'm tagged as Marr's line into Headquarters. You're getting some of that. You're sitting still and I was hiking up to Puma Lake for no good reason except to have a deer carcass planted in the back of my car and have a game warden nick me with it.'

Marcus stood up very slowly, knotting his fists at his sides. His heavy grey eyes opened very wide. His big nose was white at the nostrils.

'Nobody here'd go *that* far, Sam.'

Delaguerra shook his head. 'I don't think so either. But they could take a hint to send me up there. And somebody outside the department could do the rest.'

Pete Marcus sat down again. He picked up one of the pointed bank pens and flipped it viciously at the round straw cushion. The point stuck, quivered, broke, and the pen rattled to the floor.

'Listen,' he said thickly, not looking up, 'this is a job to me. That's all it is. A living. I don't have any ideals about this police work like you have. Say the word and I'll heave the goddamn badge in the old boy's puss.'

Delaguerra bent down, punched him in the ribs. 'Skip it, copper. I've got ideas. Go on home and get drunk.'

He opened the door and went out quickly, walked along a marble-faced corridor to a place where it widened into an alcove with three doors. The middle one said: CHIEF OF DETECTIVES. ENTER. Delaguerra went into a small reception room with a plain railing across it. A police stenographer behind the railing looked up, then jerked his head at an inner door. Delaguerra opened a gate in the railing and knocked at the inner door, then went in.

Two men were in the big office. Chief of Detectives Tod McKim sat behind a heavy desk, looked at Delaguerra hard-eyed as he came in. He was a big, loose man who had gone saggy. He had a long, petulantly melancholy face. One of his eyes was not quite straight in his head.

The man who sat in a round-backed chair at the end of the desk was dandyishly dressed, wore spats. A pearl-grey hat and grey gloves and an ebony cane lay beside him on another chair. He had a shock of soft white hair, and a handsome dissipated face kept pink by constant massaging. He smiled at Delaguerra, looked vaguely amused and ironical, smoked a cigarette in a long amber holder.

Delaguerra sat down opposite McKim. Then he looked at the white-haired man briefly and said: 'Good evening, Commissioner.'

Commissioner Drew nodded off handedly, didn't speak.

McKim leaned forward and clasped blunt, nail-chewed fingers on the shiny desk top. He said quietly: 'Took your time reporting back. Find anything?'

Delaguerra stared at him, a level expressionless stare.

'I wasn't meant to – except maybe a doe carcass in the back of my car.'

Nothing changed in McKim's face. Not a muscle of it moved. Drew dragged a pink and polished fingernail across the front of his throat and made a tearing sound with his tongue and teeth.

'That's no crack to be makin' at your boss, lad.'

Delaguerra kept on looking at McKim, waited. McKim spoke slowly, sadly: 'You've got a good record, Delaguerra. Your grandfather was one of the best sheriffs this county ever had. You've blown a lot of dirt on it today. You're charged with violating game laws, interfering with a Toluca County officer in the performance of his duty, and resisting arrest. Got anything to say to all that?'

Delaguerra said tonelessly: 'Is there a tag out for me?'

McKim shook his head very slowly. 'It's a department charge. There's no formal complaint. Lack of evidence, I guess.' He smiled dryly, without humour.

Delaguerra said quietly: 'In that case I guess you'll want my badge.'

McKim nodded, silent. Drew said: 'You're a little quick on the trigger. Just a shade fast on the snap-up.'

Delaguerra took his badge out, rubbed it on his sleeve, looked at it, pushed it across the smooth wood of the desk.

'Okay, Chief,' he said very softly. 'My blood is Spanish, pure Spanish. Not nigger-Mex and not Yaqui-Mex. My grandfather would have handled a situation like this with fewer words and more powder smoke, but that doesn't mean I think it's funny. I've been deliberately framed into this spot because I was a close friend of Donegan Marr once. You know and I know that never counted for anything on the job. The Commissioner and his political backers may not feel so sure.'

Drew stood up suddenly. 'By God, you'll not talk like that to me,' he yelped.

Delaguerra smiled slowly. He said nothing, didn't look towards Drew at all. Drew sat down again, scowling, breathing hard.

After a moment McKim scooped the badge into the middle drawer of his desk and got to his feet.

'You're suspended for a board, Delaguerra. Keep in touch with me.' He went out of the room quickly, by the inner door, without looking back.

Delaguerra pushed his chair back and straightened his hat on his head. Drew cleared his throat, assumed a conciliatory smile and said: 'Maybe I was a little hasty myself. The Irish in me. Have no hard feelings. The lesson you're learning is something we've all had to learn. Might I give you a word of advice?'

Delaguerra stood up, smiled at him, a small dry smile that moved the corners of his mouth and left the rest of his face wooden.

'I know what it is, Commissioner. Lay off the Marr case.'

Drew laughed, good-humoured again. 'Not exactly. There isn't any Marr case. Imlay has admitted the shooting, through his attorney, claiming self-defence. He's to surrender in the morning. No, my advice was something else. Go back to Toluca County and tell the warden you're sorry. I think that's all that's needed. You might try it and see.'

Delaguerra moved quietly to the door and opened it. Then he looked back with a sudden flashing grin that showed all his white teeth.

'I know a crook when I see one, Commissioner. He's been paid for his trouble already.'

He went out. Drew watched the door close shut with a faint whoosh, a dry click. His face was stiff with rage. His pink skin had turned a doughy grey. His hand shook furiously, holding the amber holder, and ash fell on the knee of his immaculate knife-edged trousers.

'By God,' he said rigidly, in the silence, 'you may be a damn smooth Spaniard. You may be smooth as plate glass – but you're a hell of a lot easier to poke a hole through!'

He rose, awkward with anger, brushed the ashes from his trousers carefully and reached a hand out for hat and cane. The manicured fingers of the hand were trembling.

8

Newton Street, between Third and Fourth, was a block of cheap clothing stores, pawnshops, arcades of slot machines, mean hotels in front of which furtive-eyed men slid words delicately along their cigarettes, without moving their lips. Midway of the block a jutting wooden sign on a canopy said, STOLL'S BILLIARD PARLOURS. Steps went down from the sidewalk edge. Delaguerra went down the steps.

It was almost dark in the front of the poolroom. The tables were sheeted, the cues racked in rigid lines. But there was light far at the back, hard white light against which clustered heads and shoulders were silhouetted. There was noise, wrangling, shouting of odds. Delaguerra went towards the light.

Suddenly, as if at a signal, the noise stopped and out of the silence came the sharp click of balls, the dull thud of cue ball against cushion after cushion, the final click of a three-bank cannon. Then the noise flared up again.

Delaguerra stopped beside a sheeted table and got a ten-dollar bill from his wallet, got a small gummed label from a pocket in the wallet. He wrote on it: 'Where is Joe?' pasted it to the bill, folded the bill in four. He went on to the fringe of the crowd and inched his way through until he was close to the table.

A tall, pale man with an impassive face and neatly parted brown hair was chalking a cue, studying the set-up on the table. He leaned over, bridged with strong white fingers. The betting ring noise dropped like a stone. The tall man made a smooth, effortless three-cushion shot.

A chubby-faced man on a high stool intoned: 'Forty for Chill. Eight's the break.'

The tall man chalked his cue again, looked around idly. His eyes passed over Delaguerra without sign. Delaguerra stepped closer to him, said: 'Back yourself, Max? Five-spot against the next shot.'

The tall man nodded. 'Take it.'

Delaguerra put the folded bill on the edge of the table. A youth in a striped shirt reached for it. Max Chill blocked him off without seeming to, tucked the bill in a pocket of his vest, said tonelessly: 'Five bet,' and bent to make another shot.

It was a clean crisscross at the top of the table, a hairline shot. There was a lot of applause. The tall man handed his cue to his helper in the striped shirt, said: 'Time out. I got to go a place.'

He went back through the shadows, through a door marked MEN. Delaguerra lit a cigarette, looked around at the usual Newton Street riffraff. Max Chill's opponent, another tall, pale, impassive man, stood beside the marker and talked to him without looking at him. Near them, alone and supercilious, a very good-looking Filipino in a smart tan suit was puffing at a chocolate-coloured cigarette.

Max Chill came back to the table, reached for his cue, chalked it. He reached a hand into his vest, said lazily: 'Owe you five, buddy,' passed a folded bill to Delaguerra.

He made three cannons in a row, almost without stopping. The marker said: 'Forty-four for Chill. Twelve's the break.'

Two men detached themselves from the edge of the crowd, started towards the entrance. Delaguerra fell in behind them, followed them among the sheeted tables to the foot of the steps. He stopped there, unfolded the bill in his hand, read the address scribbled on the label under his question. He crumpled the bill in his hand, started it towards his pocket.

Something hard poked into his back. A twangy voice like a plucked banjo string said: 'Help a guy out, huh?'

Delaguerra's nostrils quivered, got sharp. He looked up the steps at the legs of the two men ahead, at the reflected glare of street lights.

'Okay,' the twangy voice said grimly.

Delaguerra dropped sidewise, twisting in the air. He shot a snakelike arm back. His hand grabbed an ankle as he fell. A swept gun missed his head, cracked the point of his shoulder and sent a dart of pain down his left arm. There was hard hot breathing. Something without force slammed his straw hat. There was a thin tearing snarl close to him. He rolled, twisted the ankle, tucked a knee under him and lunged up. He was on his feet, catlike, lithe. He threw the ankle away from him, hard.

The Filipino in the tan suit hit the floor with his back. A gun wobbled up. Delaguerra kicked it out of a small brown hand and it skidded under a table. The Filipino lay still on his back, his head straining up, his snap-brim hat still glued to his oily hair.

At the back of the poolroom the three-cushion match went on peacefully. If anyone noticed the scuffling sound, at least no one moved to investigate. Delaguerra jerked a thonged blackjack from his hip pocket, bent over. The Filipino's tight brown face cringed.

'Got lots to learn. On the feet, baby.'

Delaguerra's voice was chilled but casual. The dark man scrambled up, lifted his arms, then his left hand snaked for his right shoulder. The blackjack knocked it down, with a careless flip of Delaguerra's wrist. The brown man screamed thinly, like a hungry kitten.

Delaguerra shrugged. His mouth moved in a sardonic grin.

'Stick-up, huh? Okay, yellowpuss, some other time. I'm busy now. Dust!'

The Filipino slid back among the tables, crouched down. Delaguerra shifted the blackjack to his left hand, shot his right to a gun butt. He stood for a moment like that, watching the Filipino's eyes. Then he turned and went quickly up the steps, out of sight.

The brown man darted forward along the wall, crept under the table for his gun.

9

Joey Chill, who jerked the door open, held a short, worn gun without a foresight. He was a small man, hardbitten, with a tight, worried face. He needed a shave and a clean shirt. A harsh animal smell came out of the room behind him.

He lowered the gun, grinned sourly, stepped back into the room.

'Okay, copper. Took your sweet time gettin' here.'

Delaguerra went in and shut the door. He pushed his straw hat far back on his wiry hair, and looked at Joey Chill without any expression. He said: 'Am I supposed to remember the address of every punk in town? I had to get it from Max.'

The small man growled something and went and lay down on the bed, shoved his gun under the pillow. He clasped his hands behind his head and blinked at the ceiling.

'Got a C-note on you, copper?'

Delaguerra jerked a straight chair in front of the bed and

straddled it. He got his bulldog pipe out, filled it slowly, look-ing with distaste at the shut window, the chipped enamel of the bed frame, the dirty, tumbled bedclothes, the wash bowl in the corner with two smeared towels hung over it, the bare dresser with half a bottle of gin planked on top of the Gideon Bible.

'Holed up?' he inquired, without much interest.

'I'm hot, copper. I mean I'm hot. I got something, see. It's worth a C-note.'

Delaguerra put his pouch away slowly, indifferently, held a lighted match to his pipe, puffed with exasperating leisure. The small man on the bed fidgeted, watching him with side-long looks. Delaguerra said slowly: 'You're a good stooly, Joey. I'll always say that for you. But a hundred bucks is im-portant money to a copper.'

'Worth it, guy. If you like the Marr killing well enough to want to break it right.'

Delaguerra's eyes got steady and very cold. His teeth clamped on the pipe stem. He spoke very quietly, very grimly.

'I'll listen, Joey. I'll pay if it's worth it. It better be right, though.'

The small man rolled over on his elbow. 'Know who the girl was with Imlay in those pyjama-pyjama snaps?'

'Know her name,' Delaguerra said evenly. 'I haven't seen the pictures.'

'Stella La Motte's a hoofer name. Real name Stella Chill. My kid sister.'

Delaguerra folded his arms on the back of the chair. 'That's nice,' he said. 'Go on.'

'She framed him, copper. Framed him for a few bindles of heroin from a slant-eyed Flip.'

'Flip?' Delaguerra spoke the word swiftly, harshly. His face was tense now.

'Yeah, a little brown brother. A looker, a neat dresser, a snow peddler. A goddamn dodo. Name, Toribo. They call him the Caliente Kid. He had a place across the hall from Stella. He got to feedin' her the stuff. Then he works her into the frame. She puts heavy drops in Imlay's liquor and he passes out. She lets the Flip in to shoot pictures with a Minné camera. Cute, huh? . . . And then, just like a broad, she gets sorry and spills the whole thing to Max and me.'

Delaguerra nodded, silent, almost rigid.

The little man grinned sharply, showed his small teeth. 'What do I do? I take a plant on the Flip. I live in his shadow, copper. And after a while I tail him bang into Dave Aage's skyline apartment in the Vendome . . . I guess that rates a yard.'

Delaguerra nodded slowly, shook a little ash into the palm of his hand and blew it off. 'Who else knows this?'

'Max. He'll back me up, if you handle him right. Only he don't want any part of it. He don't play those games. He gave Stella dough to leave town and signed off. Because those boys are tough.'

'Max couldn't know where you followed the Filipino to, Joey.'

The small man sat up sharply, swung his feet to the floor. His face got sullen.

'I'm not kidding you, copper. I never have.'

Delaguerra said quietly: 'I believe you, Joey. I'd like more proof, though. What do you make of it?'

The little man snorted. 'Hell, it sticks up so hard it hurts. Either the Flip's working for Masters and Aage before or he makes a deal with them after he gets the snaps. Then Marr gets the pictures and it's a cinch he don't get them unless they say so and he don't know they had them. Imlay was running for judge, on their ticket. Okay, he's their punk, but he's still a punk. It happens he's a guy who drinks and has a nasty temper. That's known.'

Delaguerra's eyes glistened a little. The rest of his face was like carved wood. The pipe in his mouth was as motionless as though set in cement.

Joey Chill went on, with his sharp little grin: 'So they deal the big one. They get the pictures to Marr without Marr's knowing where they came from. Then Imlay gets tipped off who has them, what they are, that Marr is set to put the squeeze on him. What would a guy like Imlay do? He'd go hunting, copper – and Big John Masters and his sidekick would eat the ducks.'

'Or the venison,' Delaguerra said absently.

'Huh? Well, does it rate?'

Delaguerra reached for his wallet, shook the money out of it, counted some bills on his knee. He rolled them into a tight wad and flipped them on to the bed.

'I'd like a line to Stella pretty well, Joey. How about it?'

The small man stuffed the money in his shirt pocket, shook his head. 'No can do. You might try Max again. I think she's left town, and me, I'm doin' that too, now I've got the scratch. Because those boys are tough like I said – and maybe I didn't tail so good. . . . Because some mug's been tailin' me.' He stood up, yawned, added: 'Snort of gin?'

Delaguerra shook his head, watched the little man go over to the dresser and lift the gin bottle, pour a big dose into a thick glass. He drained the glass, started to put it down.

Glass tinkled at the window. There was a sound like the loose slap of a glove. A small piece of the window glass dropped to the bare stained wood beyond the carpet, almost at Joey Chill's feet.

The little man stood quite motionless for two or three seconds. Then the glass fell from his hand, bounced and rolled against the wall. Then his legs gave. He went down on his side, slowly rolled slowly over on his back.

Blood began to move sluggishly down his cheek from a hole over his left eye. It moved faster. The hole got large and red. Joey Chill's eyes looked blankly at the ceiling, as if those things no longer concerned him at all.

Delaguerra slipped quietly down out of the chair to his hands and knees. He crawled along the side of the bed, over to the wall by the window, reached out from there and groped inside Joey Chill's shirt. He held fingers against his heart for a little while, took them away, shook his head. He squatted down low, took his hat off, and pushed his head up very carefully until he could see over a lower corner of the window.

He looked at the high blank wall of a storage warehouse, across an alley. There were scattered windows in it, high up, none of them lighted. Delaguerra pulled his head down again, said quietly, under his breath: 'Silenced rifle, maybe. And very sweet shooting.'

His hand went forward again, diffidently, took the little roll of bills from Joey Chill's shirt. He went back along the wall to the door, still crouched, reached up and got the key from the door, opened it, straightened and stepped through quickly, locked the door from the outside.

He went along a dirty corridor and down four flights of steps to a narrow lobby. The lobby was empty. There was a desk and a bell on it, no one behind it. Delaguerra stood behind the plate-glass street door and looked across the street at a frame rooming-house where a couple of old men rocked on the porch, smoking. They looked very peaceful. He watched them for a couple of minutes.

He went out, searched both sides of the block quickly with sharp glances, walked along beside parked cars to the next corner. Two blocks over he picked up a cab and rode back to Stoll's Billiard Parlours in Newton Street.

Lights were lit all over the poolroom now. Balls clicked and spun, players weaved in and out of a thick haze of cigarette smoke. Delaguerra looked around, then went to where a chubby-faced man sat on a high stool beside a cash register.

'You Stoll?'

The chubby-faced man nodded.

'Where did Max Chill get to?'

'Long gone, brother. They only played a hundred up. Home, I guess.'

'Where's home?'

The chubby-faced man gave him a swift, flickering glance that passed like a finger of light.

'I wouldn't know.'

Delaguerra lifted a hand to the pocket where he carried his badge. He dropped it again – tried not to drop it too quickly. The chubby-faced man grinned.

'Flatty, eh? Okay, he lives at the Mansfield, three blocks west on Grand.'

10

Cefarino Toribo, the good-looking Filipino in the well-cut tan suit, gathered two dimes and three pennies off the counter in the telegraph office, smiled at the bored blonde who was waiting on him.

'That goes out right away, Sugar?'

She glanced at the message icily. 'Hotel Mansfield? Be there in twenty minutes – and save the sugar.'

'Okay, Sugar.'

Toribo dawdled elegantly out of the office. The blonde spiked the message with a jab, said over her shoulder: 'Guy must be nuts. Sending a wire to a hotel three blocks away.'

Cefarino Toribo strolled along Spring Street, trailing smoke over his neat shoulder from a chocolate-coloured cigarette. At Fourth he turned west, went three blocks more, turned into the side entrance of the Mansfield, by the barber shop. He went up some marble steps to a mezzanine, along the back of a writing room and up carpeted steps to the third floor. He passed the elevators and swaggered down a long corridor to the end, looking at the numbers on doors.

He came back halfway to the elevators, sat down in an open space where there was a pair of windows on the court, a glass-topped table and chairs. He lit a fresh cigarette from his stub, leaned back and listened to the elevators.

He leaned forward sharply whenever one stopped at that floor, listening for steps. The steps came in something over ten minutes. He stood up and went to the corner of the wall where the widened out space began. He took a long thin gun out from under his right arm, transferred it to his right hand, held it down against the wall beside his leg.

A squat, pockmarked Filipino in bellhop's uniform came along the corridor, carrying a small tray. Toribo made a hissing noise, lifted the gun. The squat Filipino whirled. His mouth opened and his eyes bulged at the gun.

Toribo said: 'What room, punk?'

The squat Filipino smiled very nervously, placatingly. He came close, showed Toribo a yellow envelope on his tray. The figures 338 were pencilled on the window of the envelope.

'Put it down,' Toribo said calmly.

The squat Filipino put the telegram on the table. He kept his eyes on the gun.

'Beat it,' Toribo said. 'You put it under the door, see?'

The squat Filipino ducked his round black head, smiled nervously again, and went away very quickly towards the elevators.

Toribo put the gun in his jacket pocket, took out a folded white paper. He opened it very carefully, shook glistening white powder from it on to the hollow place formed between his left thumb and forefinger when he spread his hand. He sniffed the powder sharply up his nose, took out a flame-coloured silk handkerchief and wiped his nose.

He stood still for a little while. His eyes got the dullness of slate, and the skin on his brown face seemed to tighten over his high cheekbones. He breathed audibly between his teeth.

He picked up the yellow envelope and went along the corridor to the end, stopped in front of the last door, knocked.

A voice called out. He put his lips close to the door, spoke in a high-pitched, very deferential voice.

'Mail for you, sar.'

Bedsprings creaked. Steps came across the floor inside. A key turned and the door opened. Toribo had his thin gun out again by this time. As the door opened he stepped swiftly into the opening, sidewise, with a graceful sway of his hips. He put the muzzle of the thin gun against Max Chill's abdomen.

'Back up!' he snarled, and his voice now had the metallic twang of a plucked banjo string.

Max Chill backed away from the gun. He backed across the room to the bed, sat down on the bed when his legs struck the side of it. Springs creaked and a newspaper rustled. Max Chill's pale face under the neatly parted brown hair had no expression at all.

Toribo shut the door softly, snapped the lock. When the door latch snapped, Max Chill's face suddenly became a sick face. His lips began to shake, kept on shaking.

Toribo said mockingly, in his twangy voice: 'You talk to the cops, huh? *Adíos.*'

The thin gun jumped in his hand, kept on jumping. A little pale smoke lisped from the muzzle. The noise the gun made was no louder than a hammer striking a nail or knuckles rapping sharply on wood. It made that noise seven times.

Max Chill lay down on the bed very slowly. His feet stayed on the floor. His eyes went blank, and his lips parted and a pinkish froth seethed on them. Blood showed in several places on the front of his loose shirt. He lay quite still on his back and looked at the ceiling with his feet touching the floor and the pink froth bubbling on his blue lips.

Toribo moved the gun to his left hand and put it away under his arm. He sidled over to the bed and stood beside it, looking down at Max Chill. After a while the pink froth stopped bubbling and Max Chill's face became the quiet, empty face of a dead man.

Toribo went back to the door, opened it, started to back out, his eyes still on the bed. There was a stir of movement behind him.

He started to whirl, snatching a hand up. Something looped at his head. The floor tilted queerly before his eyes, rushed up at his face. He didn't know when it struck his face.

Delaguerra kicked the Filipino's legs into the room, out of the way of the door. He shut the door, locked it, walked stiffly over to the bed, swinging a thonged cosh at his side. He stood beside the bed for quite a long time. At last he said under his breath: 'They clean up. Yeah – they clean up.'

He went back to the Filipino, rolled him over and went through his pockets. There was a well-lined wallet without any identification, a gold lighter set with garnets, a gold cigarette case, keys, a gold pencil and knife, the flame coloured handkerchief, loose money, two guns and spare clips for them, and five bundles of heroin powder in the ticket pocket of the tan jacket.

He left it thrown around on the floor, stood up. The Filipino breathed heavily, with his eyes shut, a muscle twitching in one cheek. Delaguerra took a coil of thin wire out of his pocket and wired the brown man's wrists behind him. He dragged him over to the bed, sat him up against the leg, looped a strand of the wire around his neck and around the bedpost. He tied the flame-coloured handkerchief to the looped wire.

He went into the bathroom and got a glass of water and threw it into the Filipino's face as hard as he could throw it.

Toribo jerked, gagged sharply as the wire caught his neck. His eyes jumped open. He opened his mouth to yell.

Delaguerra jerked the wire taut against the brown throat. The yell was cut off as though by a switch. There was a strained anguished gurgle. Toribo's mouth drooled.

Delaguerra let the wire go slack again and put his head down close to the Filipino's head. He spoke to him gently, with a dry, very deadly gentleness.

'You want to talk to me, spig. Maybe not right away, maybe not even soon. But after a while you want to talk to me.'

The Filipino's eyes rolled yellowly. He spat. Then his lips came together, tight.

Delaguerra smiled a faint, grim smile. 'Tough boy,' he said softly. He jerked the handkerchief back, held it tight and hard, biting into the brown throat above the Adam's apple.

The Filipino's legs began to jump on the floor. His body moved in sudden lunges. The brown of his face became a thick congested purple. His eyes bulged, shot with blood.

Delaguerra let the wire go loose again.

The Filipino gasped air into his lungs. His head sagged, then jerked back against the bedpost. He shook with a chill.

'*Sí* . . . I talk,' he breathed.

II

When the bell rang Ironhead Toomey very carefully put a black ten down on a red jack. Then he licked his lips and put all the cards down and looked around towards the front door of the bungalow, through the dining-room arch. He stood up slowly, a big brute of a man with loose grey hair and a big nose.

In the living-room beyond the arch a thin blonde girl was lying on a davenport, reading a magazine under a lamp with a torn red shade. She was pretty, but too pale, and her thin, high-arched eyebrows gave her face a startled look. She put the magazine down and swung her feet to the floor and looked at Ironhead Toomey with sharp, sudden fear in her eyes.

Toomey jerked his thumb silently. The girl stood up and went very quickly through the arch and through a swing door into the kitchen. She shut the swing door slowly, so that it made no noise.

The bell rang again, longer. Toomey shoved his white-socked feet into carpet slippers, hung a pair of glasses on his big nose, took a revolver off a chair beside him. He picked a crumpled newspaper off the floor and arranged it loosely in front of the gun, which he held in his left hand. He strolled unhurriedly to the front door.

He was yawning as he opened it, peering with sleepy eyes through the glasses at the tall man who stood on the porch.

'Okay,' he said wearily. 'Talk it up.'

Delaguerra said: 'I'm a police officer. I want to see Stella La Motte.'

Ironhead Toomey put an arm like a Yule log across the door frame and leaned solidly against it. His expression remained bored.

'Wrong dump, copper. No broads here.'

Delaguerra said: 'I'll come in and look.'

Toomey said cheerfully: 'You will – like hell.'

Delaguerra jerked a gun out of his pocket very smoothly and swiftly, smashed it at Toomey's left wrist. The newspaper and the big revolver fell down on the floor of the porch. Toomey's face got a less bored expression.

'Old gag,' Delaguerra snapped. 'Let's go in.'

Toomey shook his left wrist, took his other arm off the door frame and swung hard at Delaguerra's jaw. Delaguerra moved his head about four inches. He frowned, made a disapproving noise with his tongue and lips.

Toomey dived at him. Delaguerra sidestepped and chopped the gun at a big grey head. Toomey landed on his stomach, half in the house and half out on the porch. He grunted, planted his hands firmly and started to get up again, as if nothing had hit him.

Delaguerra kicked Toomey's gun out of the way. A swing door inside the house made a light sound. Toomey was up on one knee and one hand as Delaguerra looked towards the noise. He took a swing at Delaguerra's stomach, hit him. Delaguerra grunted and hit Toomey on the head again, hard. Toomey shook his head, growled: 'Coshin' me is a waste of time, bo.'

He dived sideways, got hold of Delaguerra's leg, jerked the leg off the floor. Delaguerra sat down on the boards of the porch, jammed in the doorway. His head hit the side of the doorway, dazed him.

The thin blonde rushed through the arch with a small automatic in her hand. She pointed it at Delaguerra, said furiously: 'Reach, damn you!'

Delaguerra shook his head, started to say something, then caught his breath as Toomey twisted his foot. Toomey set his teeth hard and twisted the foot as if he was all alone in the world with it and it was his foot and he could do what he liked with it.

Delaguerra's head jerked back again and his face got white. His mouth twisted into a harsh grimace of pain. He heaved up, grabbed Toomey's hair with his left hand, dragged the big head up and over until his chin came up, straining. Delaguerra smashed the barrel of his Colt on the skin.

Toomey became limp, an inert mass, fell across his legs and pinned him to the floor. Delaguerra couldn't move. He was propped on the floor on his right hand, trying to keep from being pushed flat by Toomey's weight. He couldn't get his right hand with the gun in it off the floor. The blonde was closer to him now, wild-eyed, white-faced with rage.

Delaguerra said in a spent voice: 'Don't be a fool, Stella. Joey —'

The blonde's face was unnatural. Her eyes were unnatural, with small pupils, a queer flat glitter in them.

'Cops!' she almost screamed. 'Cops! God, how I hate cops!'

The gun in her hand crashed. The echoes of it filled the room, went out of the open front door, died against the high-board fence across the street.

A sharp blow like the blow of a club hit the left side of Delaguerra's head. Pain filled his head. Light flared – blinding white light that filled the world. Then it was dark. He fell soundlessly, into bottomless darkness.

12

Light came back as a red fog in front of his eyes. Hard, bitter pain racked the side of his head, his whole face, ground in his teeth. His tongue was hot and thick when he tried to move it. He tried to move his hands. They were far away from him, not his hands at all.

Then he opened his eyes and the red fog went away and he was looking at a face. It was a big face, very close to him, a huge face. It was fat and had sleek blue jowls and there was a cigar with a bright band in a grinning, thick-lipped mouth. The face chuckled. Delaguerra closed his eyes again and the pain washed over him, submerged him. He passed out.

Seconds, or years, passed. He was looking at the face again. He heard a thick voice.

'Well, he's with us again. A pretty tough lad at that.'

The face came closer, the end of the cigar glowed cherry-red. Then he was coughing rackingly, gagging on smoke. The side of his head seemed to burst open. He felt fresh blood slide down his cheekbone, tickling the skin, then slide over stiff dried blood that had already caked on his face.

'That fixes him up swell,' the thick voice said.

Another voice with a touch of brogue to it said something gentle and obscene. The big face whirled towards the sound, snarling.

Delaguerra came wide awake then. He saw the room clearly, saw the four people in it. The big face was the face of Big John Masters.

The thin blonde girl was hunched on one end of the daven-port, staring at the floor with a doped expression, her arms stiff at her sides, her hands out of sight in the cushions.

Dave Aage had his long lank body propped against a wall beside a curtained window. His wedge-shaped face looked bored. Commissioner Drew was on the other end of the daven-port, under the frayed lamp. The light made silver in his hair. His blue eyes were very bright, very intent.

There was a shiny gun in Big John Masters' hand. Dela-guerra blinked at it, started to get up. A hard hand jerked at his chest, jarred him back. A wave of nausea went over him. The thick voice said harshly: 'Hold it, pussyfoot. You've had your fun. This is our party.'

Delaguerra licked his lips, said: 'Give me a drink of water.'

Dave Aage stood away from the wall and went through the dining-room arch. He came back with a glass, held it to Delaguerra's mouth. Delaguerra drank.

Masters said: 'We like your guts, copper. But you don't use them right. It seems you're a guy that can't take a hint. That's too bad. That makes you through. Get me?'

The blonde turned her head and looked at Delaguerra with heavy eyes, looked away again. Aage went back to his wall. Drew began to stroke the side of his face with quick nervous fingers, as if Delaguerra's bloody head made his own face hurt.

Delaguerra said slowly: 'Killing me will just hang you a little higher, Masters. A sucker on the big time is still a sucker. You've had two men killed already for no reason at all. You don't even know what you're trying to cover.'

The big man swore harshly, jerked the shiny gun up, then lowered it slowly, with a heavy leer. Aage said indolently: 'Take it easy, John. Let him speak his piece.'

Delaguerra said in the same slow, careless voice: 'The lady over there is the sister of the two men you've had killed. She told them her story, about framing Imlay, who got the pictures, how they got to Donegan Marr. Your little Filipino hood has done some singing. I got the general idea all right. You couldn't be sure Imlay would kill Marr. Maybe Marr would get Imlay. It would work out all right either way. Only, if Imlay did kill Marr, the case had to be broken fast. That's where you slipped. You started to cover up before you really knew what happened.'

Masters said harshly: 'Crummy, copper, crummy. You're wasting my time.'

The blonde turned her head towards Delaguerra, towards Masters' back. There was hard green hate in her eyes now. Delaguerra shrugged very slightly, went on: 'It was routine stuff for you to put killers on the Chill brothers. It was routine stuff to get me off the investigation, get me framed, and suspended because you figured I was on Marr's payroll. But it wasn't routine when you couldn't find Imlay – and that crowded you.'

Masters' hard black eyes got wide and empty. His thick neck swelled. Aage came away from the wall a few feet and stood rigidly. After a moment Masters snapped his teeth, spoke very quietly: 'That's a honey, copper. Tell us about that one.'

Delaguerra touched his smeared face with the tips of two fingers, looked at the fingers. His eyes were depthless, ancient.

'Imlay is dead, Masters. He was dead before Marr was killed.'

The room was very still. Nobody moved in it. The four people Delaguerra looked at were frozen with shock. After a long time Masters drew in a harsh breath and blew it out and almost whispered: 'Tell it, copper. Tell it fast, or by God I'll — '

Delaguerra's voice cut in on him coldly, without any emotion at all: 'Imlay went to see Marr all right. Why wouldn't he? He didn't know he was double-crossed. Only he went to see him last night, not today. He rode up to the cabin at Puma Lake with him, to talk things over in a friendly way. That was the gag, anyhow. Then, up there, they had their fight and Imlay got killed, got dumped off the end of the porch, got his head smashed open on some rocks. He's dead as last Christmas, in the woodshed of Marr's cabin. . . . Okay, Marr hid him and came back to town. Then today he got a phone call, mentioning the name Imlay, making a date for twelve-fifteen. What would Marr do? Stall, of course, send his office girl off to lunch, put a gun where he could reach it in a hurry. He was all set for trouble then. Only the visitor fooled him and he didn't use the gun.'

Masters said gruffly: 'Hell, man, you're just cracking wise. You couldn't know all those things.'

He looked back at Drew. Drew was grey-faced, taut. Aage came a little farther away from the wall and stood close to Drew. The blonde girl didn't move a muscle.

Delaguerra said wearily: 'Sure, I'm guessing, but I'm guessing to fit the facts. It had to be like that. Marr was no slouch with a gun and he was on edge, all set. Why didn't he get a shot in? Because it was a woman that called on him.'

He lifted an arm, pointed at the blonde. 'There's your killer. She loved Imlay even though she framed him. She's a junky and junkies are like that. She got sad and sorry and she went after Marr herself. Ask her!'

The blonde stood up in a smooth lunge. Her right hand jerked up from the cushions with a small automatic in it, the one she had shot Delaguerra with. Her green eyes were pale and empty and staring. Masters whirled around, flailed at her arm with the shiny revolver.

She shot him twice, point blank, without a flicker of hesitation. Blood spurted from the side of his thick neck, down the front of his coat. He staggered, dropped the shiny revolver, almost at Delaguerra's feet. He fell outwards towards the wall behind Delaguerra's chair, one arm groping out for the wall. His hand hit the wall and trailed down it as he fell. He crashed heavily, didn't move again.

Delaguerra had the shiny revolver almost in his hand.

Drew was on his feet yelling. The girl turned slowly towards Aage, seemed to ignore Delaguerra. Aage jerked a Luger from under his arm and knocked Drew out of the way with his arm. The small automatic and the Luger roared at the same time. The small gun missed. The girl was flung down on the davenport, her left hand clutching at her breast. She rolled her eyes, tried to lift the gun again. Then she fell sidewise on the cushions and her left hand went lax, dropped away from her breast. The front of her dress was a sudden welter of blood. Her eyes opened and shut, opened and stayed open.

Aage swung the Luger towards Delaguerra. His eyebrows were twisted up into a sharp grin of intense strain. His smoothly combed, sand-coloured hair flowed down his bony scalp as tightly as though it were painted on it.

Delaguerra shot him four times, so rapidly that the explosions were like the rattle of a machine-gun.

In the instant of time before he fell Aage's face became the thin, empty face of an old man, his eyes the vacant eyes of an idiot. Then his long body jack-knifed to the floor, the Luger still in his hand. One leg doubled under him as if there was no bone in it.

Powder smell was sharp in the air. The air was stunned by the sound of guns. Delaguerra got to his feet slowly, motioned to Drew with the shiny revolver.

'Your party, Commissioner. Is this anything like what you wanted?'

Drew nodded slowly, white-faced, quivering. He swallowed, moved slowly across the floor, past Aage's sprawled body. He looked down at the girl on the davenport, shook his head. He went over to Masters, went down on one knee, touched him. He stood up again.

'All dead, I think,' he muttered.

Delaguerra said: 'That's swell. What happened to the big boy? The bruiser?'

'They sent him away. I – I don't think they meant to kill you, Delaguerra.'

Delaguerra nodded a little. His face began to soften, the rigid lines began to go out of it. The side that was not a bloodstained mask began to look human again. He sopped at his face with a handkerchief. It came away bright red with blood. He threw it away and lightly fingered his matted hair into place. Some of it was caught in the dried blood.

'The hell they didn't,' he said.

The house was very still. There was no noise outside. Drew listened, sniffed, went to the front door and looked out. The street outside was dark, silent. He came back close to Delaguerra. Very slowly a smile worked itself on to his face.

'It's a hell of a note,' he said, 'when a commissioner of police has to be his own undercover man – and a square cop has to be framed off the force to help him.'

Delaguerra looked at him without expression. 'You want to play it that way?'

Drew spoke calmly now. The pink was back in his face. 'For the good of the department, man, and the city – and ourselves, it's the only way to play it.'

Delaguerra looked him straight in the eyes.

'I like it that way too,' he said in a dead voice. 'If it gets played – *exactly* that way.'

13

Marcus braked the car to a stop and grinned admiringly at the big tree-shaded house.

'Pretty nice,' he said. 'I could go for a long rest there myself.'

Delaguerra got out of the car slowly, as if he was stiff and very

tired. He was hatless, carried his straw under his arm. Part of the
left side of his head was shaved and the shaved part covered by a
thick pad of gauze and tape, over the stitches. A wick of wiry
black hair stuck up over one edge of the bandage, with a
ludicrous effect.

He said: 'Yeah – but I'm not staying here, sap. Wait for
me.'

He went along the path of stones that wound through the
grass. Trees speared long shadows across the lawn, through the
morning sunlight. The house was very still, with drawn blinds,
a dark wreath on the brass knocker. Delaguerra didn't go up to
the door. He turned off along another path under the windows
and went along the side of the house past the gladioli beds.

There were more trees at the back, more lawn, more flowers,
more sun and shadow. There was a pond with water lilies in it
and a big stone bullfrog. Beyond was a half-circle of lawn
chairs around an iron table with a tile top. In one of the chairs
Belle Marr sat.

She wore a black-and-white dress, loose and casual, and there
was a wide-brimmed garden hat on her chestnut hair. She sat
very still, looking into the distance across the lawn. Her face
was white. The make-up glared on it.

She turned her head slowly, smiled a dull smile, motioned to
a chair beside her. Delaguerra didn't sit down. He took his straw
from under his arm, snapped a finger at the brim, said: 'The
case is closed. There'll be inquests, investigations, threats, a lot
of people shouting their mouths off to horn in on the publicity,
that sort of thing. The papers will play it big for a while. But
underneath, on the record, it's closed. You can begin to try to
forget it.'

The girl looked at him suddenly, widened her vivid blue
eyes, looked away again, over the grass.

'Is your head very bad, Sam?' she asked softly.

Delaguerra said: 'No. It's fine. . . . What I mean is the La
Motte girl shot Masters – and she shot Donny. Aage shot her.
I shot Aage. All dead, ring around the rosy. Just how Imlay got

killed we'll not know ever, I guess. I can't see that it matters now.'

Without looking up at him Belle Marr said quietly: 'But how did you know it was Imlay up at the cabin? The paper said — ' She broke off, shuddered suddenly.

He stared woodenly at the hat he was holding. 'I didn't. I thought a woman shot Donny. It looked like a good hunch that was Imlay up at the lake. It fitted his description.'

'How did you know it was a woman . . . that killed Donny?' Her voice had a lingering, half-whispered stillness.

'I just knew.'

He walked away a few steps, stood looking at the trees. He turned slowly, came back, stood beside her chair again. His face was very weary.

'We had great times together – the three of us. You and Donny and I. Life seems to do nasty things to people. It's all gone now – all the good part.'

Her voice was still a whisper saying: 'Maybe not all gone, Sam. We must see a lot of each other, from now on.'

A vague smile moved the corners of his lips, went away again. 'It's my first frame-up,' he said quietly. 'I hope it will be my last.'

Belle Marr's head jerked a little. Her hands took hold of the arms of the chair, looked white against the varnished wood. Her whole body seemed to get rigid.

After a moment Delaguerra reached in his pocket and something gold glittered in his hand. He looked down at it dully.

'Got the badge back,' he said. 'It's not quite as clean as it was. Clean as most, I suppose. I'll try to keep it that way.' He put it back in his pocket.

Very slowly the girl stood up in front of him. She lifted her chin, stared at him with a long level stare. Her face was a mask of white plaster behind the rouge.

She said: 'My God, Sam – I begin to understand.'

Delaguerra didn't look at her face. He looked past her

shoulder at some vague spot in the distance. He spoke vaguely, distantly.

'Sure . . . I thought it was a woman because it was a small gun such as a woman would use. But not only on that account. After I went up to the cabin I knew Donny was primed for trouble and it wouldn't be that easy for a man to get the drop on him. But it was a perfect set-up for Imlay to have done it. Masters and Aage assumed he'd done it and had a lawyer phone in admitting he did it and promising to surrender him in the morning. So it was natural for anyone who didn't know Imlay was dead to fall in line. Besides, no cop would expect a woman to pick up her shells.

'After I got Joey Chill's story I thought it might be the La Motte girl. But I didn't think so when I said it in front of her. That was dirty. It got her killed, in a way. Though I wouldn't give much for her chances anyway, with that bunch.'

Belle Marr was still staring at him. The breeze blew a wisp of her hair and that was the only thing about her that moved.

He brought his eyes back from the distance, looked at her gravely for a brief moment, looked away again. He took a small bunch of keys out of his pocket, tossed them down on the table.

'Three things were tough to figure until I got completely wise. The writing on the pad, the gun in Donny's hand, the missing shells. Then I tumbled to it. He didn't die right away. He had guts and he used them to the last flicker – to protect somebody. The writing on the pad was a bit shaky. He wrote it afterwards, when he was alone, dying. He had been thinking of Imlay, and writing the name helped mess the trail. Then he got the gun out of his desk to die with it in his hand. That left the shells. I got that too, after a while.

'The shots were fired close, across the desk, and there were books on one end of the desk. The shells fell there, stayed on the desk where he could get them. He couldn't have got them off the floor. There's a key to the office on your ring. I went there last night, late. I found the shells in a humidor with his cigars.

Nobody looked for them there. You only find what you expect to find, after all.'

He stopped talking and rubbed the side of his face. After a moment he added: 'Donny did the best he could – and then he died. It was a swell job – and I'm letting him get away with it.'

Belle Marr opened her mouth slowly. A kind of babble came out of it first, then words, clear words.

'It wasn't just women, Sam. It was the kind of women he had.' She shivered. 'I'll go downtown now and give myself up.'

Delaguerra said: 'No. I told you. I was letting him get away with it. Downtown they like it the way it is. It's swell politics. It gets the city out from under the Masters–Aage mob. It puts Drew on the top for a little while, but he's too weak to last. So that doesn't matter. . . . You're not going to do anything about any of it. You're going to do what Donny used his last strength to show he wanted. You're staying out. Good-bye.'

He looked at her white shattered face once more, very quickly. Then he swung around, walked away over the lawn, past the pool with the lily pads and the stone bullfrog, along the side of the house and out to the car.

Pete Marcus swung the door open. Delaguerra got in and sat down and put his head far back against the seat, slumped down in the car and closed his eyes. He said flatly: 'Take it easy, Pete. My head hurts like hell.'

Marcus started the car and turned into the street, drove slowly back along De Neve Lane towards town. The tree-shaded house disappeared behind them. The tall trees finally hid it.

When they were a long way from it Delaguerra opened his eyes again.

BY THE SAME AUTHOR

TITLES PUBLISHED AND FORTHCOMING

The Big Sleep

'A book to be read at a sitting' – *Sunday Times*

Farewell, My Lovely

'His first masterpiece ... every character and background is realised with an abrupt and stunning insight' – Gavin Lambert

The High Window

'Chandler is a serious writer, an original stylist, creator of a character, Philip Marlowe, as immortal as Sherlock Holmes' – Anthony Burgess

Killer in the Rain

'Chandler is the most brilliant author now writing this kind of story' – Somerset Maugham

The Lady in the Lake

'Brilliant ... the story travels at exhilarating speed' – *The Times*

The Little Sister

'He is not just one more detective writer – he is a craftsman so brilliant, he has an imagination so wholly original that no consideration of modern American literature ought, I think, to exclude him' – Elizabeth Bowen

The Long Good-Bye

'This book has the hardness and sharpness in viewing places and things that is characteristic of the best Chandler' – Julian Symons

and

Pearls are a Nuisance

Playback

Trouble is My Business

FOR THE BEST IN PAPERBACKS, LOOK FOR THE

PENGUIN CLASSIC CRIME

The Big Knockover and Other Stories Dashiell Hammett

With these sharp, spare, laconic stories, Hammett invented a new folk hero – the private eye. 'Dashiell Hammett gave murder back to the kind of people that commit it for reasons, not just to provide a corpse; and with the means at hand, not with handwrought duelling pistols, curare, and tropical fish' – Raymond Chandler

Death of a Ghost Margery Allingham

A picture painted by a dead artist leads to murder . . . and Albert Campion has to face his dearest enemy. With the skill we have come to expect from one of the great crime writers of all time, Margery Allingham weaves an enthralling web of murder, intrigue and suspense.

Fen Country Edmund Crispin

Dandelions and hearing aids, a bloodstained cat, a Leonardo drawing, a corpse with an alibi, a truly poisonous letter . . . these are just some of the unusual clues that Oxford don/detective Gervase Fen is confronted with in this sparkling collection of short mystery stories by one of the great masters of detective fiction. 'The mystery fan's ideal bedside book' – *Kirkus Reviews*

The Wisdom of Father Brown G. K. Chesterton

Twelve delightful stories featuring the world's most beloved amateur sleuth. Here Father Brown's adventures take him from London to Cornwall, from Italy to France. He becomes involved with bandits, treason, murder, curses, and an American crime-detection machine.

Five Roundabouts to Heaven John Bingham

At the heart of this novel is a conflict of human relationships ending in death. Centred around crime, the book is remarkable for its humanity, irony and insight into the motives and weaknesses of men and women, as well as for a tensely exciting plot with a surprise ending. One of the characters, considering reasons for killing, wonders whether the steps of his argument are *Five Roundabouts to Heaven*. Or do they lead to Hell? . . .'